Right Guard Grant

Ralph Henry Barbour

Illustrated by Leslie Crump

RIGHT GUARD GRANT

RALPH HENRY BARBOUR

RIGHT GUARD GRANT

THE FOOTBALL ELEVEN BOOKS

BY

Ralph Henry Barbour

LEFT END EDWARDS

LEFT TACKLE THAYER

LEFT GUARD GILBERT

CENTER RUSH ROWLAND

FULL-BACK FOSTER

QUARTER-BACK BATES

LEFT HALF HARMON

RIGHT END EMERSON

RIGHT GUARD GRANT

Then it was that Leonard had his great moment

RIGHT GUARD
GRANT

BY

RALPH HENRY BARBOUR

AUTHOR OF

LEFT END EDWARDS,
FULL-BACK FOSTER,
RIGHT END EMERSON, Etc.

ILLUSTRATED BY

LESLIE CRUMP

GROSSET & DUNLAP
PUBLISHERS   NEW YORK

Made in the United States of America

CONTENTS

CHAPTER

ILLUSTRATIONS

CHAPTER I
CAPTAIN AND COACH

Although the store had reopened for business only that morning several customers had already been in and out, and when the doorway was again darkened momentarily Russell Emerson looked up from his task of marking football trousers with merely perfunctory interest. Then, however, since the advancing figure, silhouetted flatly against the hot September sunlight of the wide-open door, looked familiar, he eased his long legs over the edge of the counter and strode to meet it.

"Hello, Cap!" greeted the visitor. The voice was unmistakable, and, now that the speaker had left the sunlight glare behind him, so too was the perspiring countenance.

"Mr. Cade!" exclaimed Russell. "Mighty glad to see you, sir. When did you get in?"

Coach Cade lifted himself to the counter and fanned himself with a faded straw hat. "About two hours ago. Unpacked, had a bath and here I am. By jove, Emerson, but it's hot!"

"Is it?"

"'Is it?'" mimicked the other. "Don't you know it is?" Then he laughed. "Guess I was a fool to get out of that bath tub, but I wanted to have a chat with you, and I'm due at Doctor McPherson's this evening." He stopped fanning his reddened face and tossed his hat atop a pile of brown canvas trousers beside him. "Johnny" Cade was short of stature, large-faced and broad in a compact way. In age he was still under thirty. He had a pleasantly mild voice that was at startling variance with his square, fighting chin, his sharp eyes and the mop of very black and bristle-like hair that always reminded Russell of a shoe brush. The mild voice continued after a moment, while the sharp eyes roamed up and down the premises. "Got things fixed up here pretty nicely," he observed commendingly. "Looks as businesslike as any sporting goods store I know. Branched out, too, haven't you?" He nodded across to where three bicycles, brave in blue-and-tan and red-and-white enamel, leaned.

1

"Yes," answered Russell. "We thought we might try those. They're just samples. 'Stick' hasn't recovered from the shock of my daring yet." Russell laughed softly. "Stick's nothing if not conservative, you know."

"Stick? Oh, yes, that's Patterson, your partner here." Mr. Cade's glance swept the spaces back of the counters.

"He's over at the express office trying to trace some goods that ought to have shown up three days ago," explained Russell. "How have you been this summer, sir?"

"Me? Oh, fine. Been working pretty hard, though." The coach's mind seemed not to be on his words, however, and he added: "Say, that blue-and-yellow wheel over there is certainly a corker. We didn't have them as fine as that when I was a kid." He got down and walked across to examine the bicycle. Russell followed.

"It is good-looking, isn't it? Better let me sell you one of those, sir. Ought to come in mighty handy following the squads around the field!"

Coach Cade grinned as he leaned the wheel back in its place with evident regret. "Gee, I suppose I'd break my silly neck if I tried to ride one of those things now. I haven't been on one of them for ten years. Sort of wish I were that much younger, though, and could run around on that, Cap!"

"You'd pick it up quickly enough," said Russell as he again perched himself on the counter. "Riding a bicycle's like skating, Mr. Cade: it comes back to you."

"Yes, I dare say," replied the other dryly. "Much the same way, I guess. Last time I tried to skate I nearly killed myself. What are you trying to do? Get a new football coach here?"

Russell laughed. "Nothing like that, sir. What we need isn't a new coach, I guess, but a new team."

"H'm, yes, that's pretty near so. I was looking over the list this morning on the train and, well—" He shrugged his broad shoulders. "Looks like building from the ground up, eh?"

"Only three left who played against Kenly."

"Three or four. Still, we have got some good material in sight, Cap. I wouldn't wonder if we had a team before the season's over." The coach's eyes twinkled, and Russell smiled in response. He had a very nice smile, a smile that lighted the quiet brown eyes and deepened the two creases leading from the corners of a firm mouth to the sides of a short nose. Russell Emerson was eighteen, a senior at Alton Academy this year and, as may have been surmised, captain of the football team.

"Seen any of the crowd lately?" asked the coach.

"No. I ran across 'Slim' once in August. He was on a sailboat trying to get up the Hudson; he and three other chaps. I don't think they ever made it."

"Just loafing, I suppose," sighed the coach. "I dare say not one of them has seen a football since spring practice ended."

"Well, I don't believe Slim had one with him," chuckled Russell. "I guess I ought to confess that I haven't done very much practicing myself, sir. I was working most of the time. Dad has a store, and he rather looks to me to give him a hand in summer."

"You don't need practice the way some of the others do," said Mr. Cade. "Well, we'll see. By the way, we're getting that fellow Renneker, from Castle City High."

"Renneker? Gordon Renneker you mean?" asked Russell in surprise.

Mr. Cade nodded. "That's the fellow. A corking good lineman, Cap. Made the Eastern All-Scholastic last year and the year before that. Played guard last season. If he's half the papers say he is he ought to fill in mighty well in Stimson's place."

"How did we happen to get him?" asked Russell interestedly.

"Oh, it's all straight, if that's what you're hinting at," was the answer. "You know I don't like 'jumpers.' They're too plaguy hard to handle, generally. Besides, there's the ethics of the thing. No, we're getting Renneker honestly. Seems that he and Cravath are acquainted, and Cravath went after him. Landed him, too, it seems. Cravath wrote me in July that Renneker would be along this fall, and just to make sure I dropped a line to Wharton, and Wharton wrote back that Renneker had registered. So I guess it's certain enough."

"Well, that's great," said Russell. "I remember reading about Gordon Renneker lots of times. If we have him on one side of Jim Newton and Smedley on the other, sir, we'll have a pretty good center trio for a start."

"Newton? Well, yes, perhaps. There's Garrick, too, you know, Cap."

"Of course, but I thought Jim—"

"He looks good, but I never like to place them until I've seen them work, Emerson. Place them seriously I mean. Of course, you have to make up a team on paper just to amuse yourself. Here's one I set down this morning. I'll bet you, though, that there won't be half of them where I've got them now when the season's three weeks old!"

Russell took the list and read it: "Gurley, Butler, Smedley, Garrick, Renneker, Wilde, Emerson, Carpenter, Goodwin, Kendall, Greenwood." He smiled. "I see you've got me down, sir. You're dead wrong in two places, though."

"Only two? Which two? Oh, yes, center. What other?"

"Well, I like 'Red' Reilly instead of, say, Kendall. And I'll bet you'll see Slim playing one end or the other before long."

Mr. Cade accepted the paper and tucked it away in a pocket again. "Well, I said this was just for amusement," he observed, untroubled. "There may be some good material coming in that we haven't heard of, too. You never know where you'll find a prize. Were any of last year's freshmen promising?"

"I don't know, sir. I didn't see much of the youngsters."

"Seen Tenney yet?"

"Yes, he blew in this morning. He's going to make a good manager, I think."

"Hope so. Did he say anything about the schedule?"

"Yes, he said it was all fixed. Hillsport came around all right. I don't see what their kick was, anyway."

4

"Wanted a later date because they held us to a tie last season," said the coach, smiling.

"Gee, any one could have tied us about the time we played Hillsport! That was during that grand and glorious slump."

"Grand and glorious indeed!" murmured the coach. "Let's hope there'll never be another half so grand! Well, I'll get along, I guess. By the way—" Mr. Cade hesitated. Then: "I hope this store isn't going to interfere too much with football, Emerson. Mustn't let it, eh? Good captains are scarce, son, and I'd hate to see one spoiled by—er—outside interests, so to speak. Don't mind my mentioning it, do you?"

"Not a mite, sir. You needn't worry. I'm putting things in shape here so that Stick can take the whole thing on his own shoulders. I'm not going to have anything to do with this shop until we've licked Kenly Hall."

"Good stuff! See you to-morrow, then. Practice at three, Cap, no matter what the weather's like. I guess a lot of those summer loafers will be the better for losing five or six pounds of fat! And about this Renneker, Cap. If you run across him it might be a good idea to sort of make yourself acquainted and—er—look after him a bit. You know what I mean. Start him off with a good impression of us, and all that."

Russell chuckled. "It's a great thing to bring a reputation with you, isn't it?" he asked.

"Eh?" The coach smiled a trifle sheepishly. "Oh, well, I don't care what you do with him," he declared. "Chuck him down the well if you like. No reason why we should toady to him, and that's a fact. I only thought that—"

"Right-o!" laughed Russell. "Leave him to me, sir. Can't sell you a bicycle then?"

"Huh," answered Mr. Cade, moving toward the door, "if you supply the team with its outfits and stuff this fall I guess you won't need to sell me a bicycle to show a profit! See you to-morrow, Cap!"

In front of the store, under the gayly-hued escutcheon bearing the legend: Sign of the Football, Mr. Cade paused to shake hands with a tall, thin youth with curly brown hair above gray eyes, a rather large nose and a broad mouth who, subsequent to the football coach's departure, entered the store hurriedly, announcing as he did so: "They can't find it, Rus! The blamed thing's just plain vanished. What'll we do? Telegraph or what?"

"I'll write them a letter," replied Russell calmly. "I dare say the stuff will show up to-morrow."

"Sure," agreed Stick Patterson sarcastically. "It's been turning up to-morrow for three days and it might as well go on turning— What was Johnny after?"

"Just wanted to talk over a few things. Give me a hand with this truck, will you? I want to get in an hour's practice before supper. Bring some more tags along. Where's the invoice? Can you see it?"

"Yes, and so could you if you weren't sitting on it. My, but it's hot over in that office! I suppose Johnny wasn't awfully enthused over the outlook, eh?"

"No-o, but he brought some good news, Stick. Ever hear of Gordon Renneker?"

"No, who's he?"

"He's a gentleman who played football last year down on Long Island with the Castle City High School team. Won everything in sight, I think."

"Who did? Runniger?"

"The team did. Renneker played guard; right guard, I guess; and got himself talked about like a moving picture hero. Some player, they say. Anyway, he's coming here this fall."

"Oh, joy! I'll bet you anything you like he'll turn out a lemon, like that chap Means, or whatever his name was, two years ago. Remember? The school got all het up about him. He was the finest thing that ever happened—until he'd been around here a couple of weeks. After that no one ever heard of him. He didn't even hold a job with the second!"

"I guess Renneker's in a different class," responded Russell. "They put him down on the All-Scholastic last fall, anyway, Stick."

"All right. Hope he turns out big. But I never saw one of these stars yet that didn't have something wrong with him. If he really could play, why, he was feeble-minded. Or if he had all his brains working smooth he had something else wrong with him. No stars in mine, thanks! Shove the ink over here. How about dressing the windows? Want me to do it?"

"Sure. Want you to do everything there is to be done, beginning with twelve o'clock midnight to-night. That's the last. Pile them up and let's get out of here. It's after five. If you'll come over to the field with me for an hour I'll buy your supper, Stick. And the exercise will do you good!"

CHAPTER II
TWO IN A TAXI

Something over eighteen hours later the morning train from New York pulled up at Alton station and disgorged a tumultuous throng of youths of all sizes and of all ages between twelve and twenty. They piled down from the day coaches and descended more dignifiedly from the two parlor cars to form a jostling, noisy mob along the narrow platform. Suit-cases, kit-bags, valises, tennis rackets, golf clubs were everywhere underfoot. Ahead, from the baggage car, trunks crashed or thudded to the trucks while an impatient conductor glanced frowningly at his watch. Behind the station the brazen clanging of the gongs on the two special trolley cars punctuated the babel, while the drivers of taxicabs and horse-drawn vehicles beckoned invitingly for trade and added their voices to the general pandemonium. Then, even as the train drew on again, the tumult lessened and the throng melted. Some few of the arrivals set forth afoot along Meadow street, having entrusted their hand luggage to friends traveling by vehicle. A great many more stormed the yellow trolley cars, greeting the grinning crews familiarly as Bill or Mike, crowding through the narrow doors and battling good-naturedly for seats. The rest, less than a score of them, patronized the cabs and carriages.

Leonard Grant was of the latter. As this was his first sight of Alton he decided that it would be wise to place the responsibility of delivering himself and a bulging suit-case to Alton Academy on the shoulders of one who knew where the Academy was, even if it was to cost a whole half-dollar! The taxi was small but capable of accommodating four passengers at least, and when Leonard had settled himself therein it became evident that the driver of the vehicle had no intention of leaving until the accommodations were more nearly exhausted. He still gesticulated and shouted, while Leonard, his suit-case up-ended between his knees, looked curiously about and tried to reconcile the sun-smitten view of cheap shops and glaring yellow brick pavement with what he had learned of Alton from the Academy catalogue. Judging solely from what he now saw, he would have concluded that the principal industries of the town were pressing clothes and supplying cheap meals. He was growing sensible of disappointment when a big kit-bag was thrust against his knees and a second passenger followed it into the cab.

"Mind if I share this with you?" asked the new arrival. He had a pleasant voice, and the inquiry was delivered in tones of the most perfect politeness, but something told Leonard that the big fellow who was making the cushion springs creak protestingly really cared not a whit whether Leonard minded or not. Leonard as courteously replied in the negative, and in doing so he had his first glimpse of his companion. He was amazingly good-looking; perhaps fine-looking would be the better term, for it was not only that his features were as regular as those on a Greek coin, but they were strong, and the smooth tanned skin almost flamboyantly proclaimed perfect health. In fact, health and physical strength fairly radiated from the chap. He was tall, wide-shouldered, deep-chested, and yet, in spite of his size, which made Leonard feel rather like a pygmy beside him, you were certain that there wasn't an ounce of soft flesh anywhere about him. He had dark eyes and, although Leonard couldn't see it just then, dark hair very carefully brushed down against a well-shaped head. He was dressed expensively but in excellent taste: rough brownish-gray tweed, a linen-colored silk shirt with collar to match, a plain brown bow-tie, a soft straw hat, brown sport shoes and brown silk socks. The watch on his wrist was plainly expensive, as were the gold-and-enamel links in his soft cuffs. What interested Leonard Grant more than these details of attire, however, was the sudden conviction that he knew perfectly well who his companion was—if only he could remember!

Meanwhile, evidently despairing of another fare, the driver climbed to his seat and set forth with loud grinding of frayed gears, cleverly manipulating the rattling cab around the end of the nearer trolley car and dodging a lumbering blue ice-wagon by a scant four inches. Then the cab settled down on the smooth pavement and flew, honking, along Meadow street.

"Are you an Alton fellow?" inquired Leonard's companion as they emerged from the jam. He spoke rather slowly, rather lazily, enunciating each word very clearly. Leonard couldn't have told why he disliked that precision of speech, but he did somehow.

9

"Yes," he answered. "And I suppose you are."

The other nodded. There was nothing really supercilious about that nod; it merely seemed to signify that in the big chap's judgment the question was not worthy a verbal reply. As he nodded he let his gaze travel over Leonard and then to the scuffed and discolored and generally disreputable suit-case, a suit-case that, unlike the kit-bag nearby, was not distinguished by bravely colored labels of travel. The inspection was brief, but it was thorough, and when it had ended Leonard knew perfectly that no detail of his appearance had been missed. He became uncomfortably conscious of his neat but well-worn Norfolk suit, his very unattractive cotton shirt, his second-season felt hat, his much-creased blue four-in-hand tie, which didn't match anything else he had on, and his battered shoes whose real condition the ten-cent shine he had acquired in the New York station couldn't disguise. It was evident to him that, with the inspection, his companion's interest in him had died a swift death. The big, outrageously good-looking youth turned his head toward the lowered window of the speeding cab and not again did he seem aware of Leonard's presence beside him.

Leonard didn't feel any resentment. The big fellow was a bit of a swell, and he wasn't. That was all there was to it. Nothing to be peeved at. Doubtless there'd be others of the same sort at the Academy, and Leonard neither expected to train with them or wanted to. What did bother him, though, was the persistent conviction that somewhere or other he had seen the big chap before, and all the way along Meadow street he stole surreptitious glances at the noble profile and racked his mind. So deep was he in this occupation that he saw little of the town; which was rather a pity, since it had become far more like his preconceived conception of it now; and the cab had entered the Meadow street gate of the Academy grounds and was passing the first of the buildings before he was aware that he had reached his destination. He would have been more interested in that first building had he known that it was Haylow Hall and that he was destined to occupy a certain room therein whose ivy-framed window stared down on him as he passed.

The driver, following custom, pulled up with disconcerting suddenness at the entrance of Academy Building, swung off his seat, threw open the door on Leonard's side and wrested the battered suit-case from between the latter's legs. Then he as swiftly transferred Leonard's half-dollar from the boy's fingers to his pocket and grabbed for the distinguished kit-bag beyond. Leonard, unceremoniously thrust into a noonday world dappled with the shadows of lazily swaying branches and quite unfamiliar, took up his bag and instinctively ascended the steps. There were other youths about him, coming down, going up or just loitering, but none heeded him. Before he reached the wide, open doorway he paused and looked back. Straight away and at a slight descent traveled a wide graveled path between spreading trees, its far end a hot blur of sunlight. At either side of the main path stretched green sward, tree dotted, to the southern and northern boundaries of the campus. Here and there a group of early arrivals were seated or stretched in the shade of the trees, coolly colorful blots against the dark green of the shadowed turf. Two other paths started off below him, diverging, one toward a handsome building which Leonard surmised to be Memorial Hall, holding the library and auditorium, the other toward the residence of the Principal, Doctor Maitland McPherson, or, in school language, "Mac." Each of these structures stood close to the confines of the campus; the other buildings were stretched right and left, toeing the transverse drive with military precision; Haylow and Lykes, dormitories, on the south flank; Academy Building in the center: Upton and Borden, dormitories, too, completing the rank. Somewhere to the rear, as Leonard recalled, must be the gymnasium and the place where they fed you; Lawrence Hall, wasn't it? Well, this looked much more like what he had expected, and he certainly approved of it.

He went on into the restful gloom of the corridor, his eyes for the moment unequal to the sudden change. Then he found the Office and took his place in the line before the counter. He had to wait while three others were disposed of, and then, just as his own turn came, he heard at the doorway the pleasant, leisurely voice of his late companion in the cab. There was another boy with him, a tall, nice-appearing chap, who was saying as they entered: "You're in Upton, with a fellow named Reilly, who plays half for us. It's a good room, Renneker, and you'll like Red, I'm sure."

"Thanks." The other's voice was noncommittal.

Leonard, moving past the desk, turned swiftly and stared with surprise and incredulity. He remembered now. Last November he had gone up to Philadelphia to see a post-season football game between a local team and an eleven from Castle City, Long Island. The visitors had won by the margin of one point after a slow and gruelling contest. Leonard's seat had been close to the visiting team's bench and a neighbor had pointed out to him the redoubtable Renneker and told him tales of the big fellow's prowess. Leonard had had several good looks at the Castle City star and had admired him, just as, later, he had admired his playing. Renneker had proved all that report had pictured him: a veritable stone wall in defense, a battering ram in attack. He had worn down two opponents, Leonard recalled, and only the final whistle had saved a third from a like fate. As Leonard had played the guard position himself that fall on his own high school team he watched Renneker's skill and science the more interestedly. And so this was Renneker! Yes, he remembered now, although in Philadelphia that day the famous player had been in togs and had worn a helmet. It is always a satisfaction to finally get the better of an obstinate memory, and for the first moment or two succeeding his victory Leonard was so immersed in that satisfaction that he failed to consider what the arrival of Gordon Renneker at Alton Academy would mean to his own football prospects. When he did give thought to that subject his spirits fell, and, rescuing his suit-case, he went out in search of Number 12 Haylow Hall with a rueful frown on his forehead.

Leonard was only seventeen, with little more than the size and weight belonging to the boy of that age, and he had told himself all along that it was very unlikely he would be able to make the Alton team that fall. But now he realized that, in spite of what he had professed to believe, he had really more than half expected to win a place on the eleven this season. After all, he had done some pretty good work last year, and the high school coach back in Loring Point had more than once assured him that by this fall he ought to be able to pit himself against many a lineman older and heavier. "Get another twenty pounds on you, Len," Tim Walsh had said once, "and there's not many that'll be able to stand up to you in the line.

I'll give you two years more, son, and then I'll be lookin' for your name in the papers. There's lots of fellows playing guard that has plenty below the neck, but you've got it above, too, see? Beef and muscle alone didn't ever win a battle. It was brains as did it. Brains and fight. And you've got both, I'll say that for you!"

And then, just a week ago, when Leonard had gone to bid Tim good-by, the little coach had said: "I'm sorry to lose you, Len, but you'll be getting a bigger chance where you're going. Sure. And you'll be getting better handlin', too. Take those big schools, why, they got trainers that knows their business, Len, and you'll be looked after close and careful. Here a fellow has to do his own trainin', which means he don't do none, in spite of all I say to him. Sure. You'll do fine, son. Well, so long. Don't put your name to nothin' without you read it first. And don't forget what I been tellin' you, Len: get 'em before they get you!"

Well, he hadn't put on that twenty pounds yet, for in spite of all his efforts during the summer—he had gone up to his uncle's farm and worked in the field and lived on the sort of food that is supposed to build bone and tissue—he was only seven pounds heavier than when he had weighed himself a year ago. And now here was this fellow Renneker to further dim his chances. Leonard sighed as he turned in at the doorway of the dormitory building. If there were eleven guards on a football team he might stand a show, he thought disconsolately, but there were only two, and one of the two would be Gordon Renneker! He wondered what his chance with the scrubs would be!

He tugged his heavy suit-case up one flight of stairs in Haylow and looked for a door bearing the numerals 12. He found it presently, cheered somewhat to observe that it was toward the campus side of the building. It was closed, and a card thumb-tacked to the center bore the inscription, "Mr. Eldred Chichester Staples." Leonard read the name a second time. That "Chichester" annoyed him. To have a roommate named Eldred might be borne, but "Chichester"— He shook his head gloomily as he turned the knob and pushed the door open. It seemed to him that life at Alton Academy wasn't starting out very well for him.

He was a bit relieved to find the room empty, although it was evident enough that Eldred Chichester Staples had already taken possession. There were brushes and toilet articles atop one of the two slim chiffoniers, books on the study table, photographs tacked to the wainscoting, a black bag reposing on a chair by the head of the left-hand bed, a pair of yellow silk pajamas exuding from it. Leonard set his own bag down and walked to the windows. There were two of them, set close together, and they looked out into the lower branches of a maple. Directly below was the brick foot-path and the gravel road—and, momentarily, the top of an automobile retreating toward the Meadow street gate. Some fortunate youth had probably arrived in the family touring car. Leonard had to set one knee on a comfortably broad window-seat to get the view, and when he turned away his knee swept something from the cushion to the floor. Rescuing it, he saw that it was a block of paper, the top sheet bearing writing done with a very soft pencil. With no intention of doing so, he read the first words: "Lines on Returning to My Alma Mater." He sniffed. So that was the sort this fellow Chichester was! Wrote poetry! Gosh! He tossed the tablet back to the window-seat. Then the desire to know how bad the effort might be prompted him to pick it up and, with a guilty glance toward the door, read further. There were many erasures and corrections, but he made out:

"Oh, classic shades that through the pleasant years
 Have sheltered me from gloomy storm and stress,
 See on my pallid cheeks the happy tears
 That tell a tale of banished loneliness."

"What sickening rot!" muttered Leonard. But he went on.

"Back to your tender arms! My tired feet
 Stand once again where they so safely stood.
 Could I want fairer haven, fate more sweet?
 Could I? *Oh, boy, I'll say I could!*"

Leonard re-read the last line doubtfully. Then he pitched the effusion violently back to the cushion.

"Huh!" he said.

CHAPTER III
ENTER MR. ELDRED CHICHESTER STAPLES

Eldred Chichester Staples had not arrived by the time Leonard had unpacked his bag. His trunk, which was to have joined him inside an hour, according to the disciple of Ananias who had accepted his claim check, had not appeared, and, since it was dinner time now, Leonard washed, re-tied his scarf, used a whisk brush rather perfunctorily and descended the stairs in search of food. It wasn't hard to find Lawrence Hall. All he had to do was follow the crowd, and, although the entire assemblage of some four hundred students was not by any means yet present, there were enough on hand to make a very good imitation of a crowd. Leonard endured some waiting before he was assigned a seat, but presently he was established at a table occupied by five others—there were seats for four more, but they weren't claimed until supper time—and was soon enjoying his first repast at Alton. The food was good and there was plenty of it, but none too much for the new boy, for his breakfast, partaken of at home before starting the first leg of his journey to New York City, was scarcely a memory. He followed the example of his right-hand neighbor and ordered "seconds" of the substantial articles of the menu and did excellently. Towards dessert he found leisure to look about him.

Lawrence Hall was big and airy and light, and although it accommodated more than twenty score, including the faculty, the tables were not crowded together and there was an agreeable aspect of space. The fellows about him appeared to be quite the usual, normal sort; although later on Leonard made the discovery that there was a certain sameness about them, somewhat as though they had been cut off the same piece of goods. This sameness was rather intangible, however; he never succeeded in determining whether it was a matter of looks, manner or voice; and I doubt if any one else could have determined. Dinner was an orderly if not a silent affair. There was an ever-continuing rattle of dishes beneath the constant hum of voices and the ripples of laughter. Once a dish fell just beyond the screen that hid the doors to the kitchen, and its crash was hailed with loud hand-clapping from every quarter. After awhile the scraping of chairs added a new note to the pleasant babel, and, contributing his own scrape, Leonard took his departure.

He had seen a notice in the corridor of Academy Building announcing the first football practice for three o'clock, and he meant to be on hand, but more than an hour intervened and he wondered how to spend it. The question was solved for him when he reached the walk that led along the front of the dormitories, for there, before the entrance of Haylow, a piled motor truck was disgorging trunks. His own proved to be among them, and he followed it upstairs and set to work. It wasn't a very large trunk, nor a very nobby one, having served his father for many years, before falling to Leonard, and he was quite satisfied that his room-mate continued to absent himself. He emptied it of his none too generous wardrobe, hung his clothes in his closet or laid them in the drawers of his chiffonier, arranged his small belongings before the mirror or on the table and finally, taking counsel of a strange youth hurrying past in the corridor, lugged the empty trunk to the store-room in the basement. Then, it now being well past the half-hour, he changed into an ancient suit of canvas, pulled on a pair of scuffed shoes and set forth for the field.

The hot weather still held, and, passing the gravel tennis courts, a wave of heat, reflected from the surface, made him gasp. The gridiron, when he reached it, proved to have suffered in many places from the fortnight of unseasonable weather and lack of rain. Half a dozen fellows, dressed for play, were laughingly squabbling for a ball near the center of the field, and their cleats, digging into the dry sod, sent up a cloud of yellow dust. Early as he was, Leonard found at least a score of candidates ahead of him. Many of them had, perhaps wisely, scorned the full regalia of football and had donned old flannel trousers in lieu of padded canvas. A perspiring youth with a very large board clip was writing busily in the scant shade of the covered stand, and a short, broadly-built man in trousers and a white running shirt, from which a pair of bronze shoulders emerged massively, was beside him. The latter was, Leonard concluded, the coach. He looked formidable, with that large countenance topped by an alarming growth of black hair, and Leonard recalled diverse tales he had heard or read of the sternness and even ferocity of professional football coaches. Evidently football at Alton Academy was going to prove more of a business than football at Loring Point High School!

This reflection was interrupted by a voice. A large youth with rather pale blue eyes that, nevertheless, had a remarkable sparkle in them had come to a stop at Leonard's elbow. "I've accumulated seventeen pounds this summer," the chap was saying, "and it cost the dad a lot of good money. And now—" his blue eyes turned from Leonard and fell disapprovingly on the sun-smitten gridiron—"now I'm going to lose the whole blamed lot in about sixty minutes." He looked to Leonard again for sympathy. Leonard smiled doubtfully. It was difficult to tell whether the stranger spoke in fun or earnest.

"If it comes off as easy as that," he replied, "I guess you don't want it." Looking more closely at the chap, he saw that, deprived of those seventeen pounds, he would probably be rather rangy; large still, but not heavy. Leonard judged that he was a backfield candidate; possibly a running half; he looked to be fast.

"I suppose not," the fellow agreed in doubtful tones. "Maybe it isn't losing the weight that worries me so much as losing it so quick. You know they say that losing a lot of weight suddenly is dangerous. Suppose it left me in an enfeebled condition!"

Now Leonard knew that the chap was joking, and he ventured a laugh. "Maybe you'd better not risk it," he said. "Why not wait until to-morrow. It might be cooler then."

"I would," replied the other gravely, "only Johnny rather leans on me, you know. I dare say he'd be altogether at a loss if I deserted him to-day. Getting things started is always a bit of a trial."

"I see. I suppose Johnny is the coach, and that's him up there." Leonard nodded in the direction of the black-haired man on the stand.

"Him or he," answered the other gently. "You're a new fellow, I take it. Fresh?"

Leonard, nettled by the correction, answered a bit stiffly, "Sophomore."

The tall youth gravely extended a hand. "Welcome," he said. "Welcome to the finest class in the school."

Leonard shook hands, his slight resentment vanishing. "I suppose that means that you're a soph, too."

The fellow nodded. "So far," he assented. Then he smiled for the first time, and after that smile Leonard liked him suddenly and thoroughly. "If you ask me that again after mid-year," he continued, "you may get a different answer. Well, I guess I'd better go up and get Johnny started. He's evidently anxious about me." He nodded once more and moved past Leonard and through the gate to the stand. Leonard had not noticed any sign of anxiety on the coach's countenance, but it wasn't to be denied that the greeting between the two was hearty. Leonard's new acquaintance seated himself at the coach's side and draped his long legs luxuriously over the back of the seat in front. The youth with the clip looked up from his writing and said something and the others threw their heads back and laughed. Leonard was positively relieved to discover that the coach could laugh like that. He couldn't be so very ferocious, after all!

The trainer appeared, followed by a man trundling a wheelbarrow laden with paraphernalia. The throng of candidates increased momentarily along the side-line and a few hardy youths, carrying coats over arms, perched themselves on the seats to look on. Leonard again turned to observe the coach and found that gentleman on his feet and extending his hand to a big chap in unstained togs. The two shook hands, and then the big fellow turned his head to look across the field, and Leonard saw that he was Gordon Renneker. A fifth member had joined the group, and him Leonard recognized as the boy who had accompanied Renneker into the office. Leonard surmised now that he was the captain: he had read the chap's name but had forgotten it. After a moment of conversation, during which the other members of the group up there seemed to be giving flattering attention to Renneker's portion, the five moved toward the field, and a minute later the business of building a football team had begun.

Coach Cade made a few remarks, doubtless not very different from those he had made at this time of year on many former occasions, was answered with approving applause and some laughter and waved a brown hand. The group of some seventy candidates dissolved, footballs trickled away from the wheelbarrow and work began. Leonard made one of a circle of fifteen or sixteen other novices who passed a ball from hand to hand and felt the sun scorching earnestly at the back of his neck. Later, in charge of a heavy youth whose name Leonard afterwards learned was Garrick, the group was conducted further down the field and was permitted to do other tricks with the ball—two balls, to be exact. They caught it on the bound, fell on it and snuggled it to their perspiring bodies and then again, while they recovered somewhat of their breath, passed it from one to another. In other portions of the field similar exercises were going on with other actors in the parts, while, down near the further goal balls were traversing the gridiron, propelled by hand or toe. Garrick was a lenient task-master, and breathing spells were frequent, and yet, even so, there were many in Leonard's squad who were just about spent when they were released to totter back to the benches and rinse their parched mouths with warm water from the carboy which, having been carefully deposited an hour ago in the shade of the wheelbarrow, was now enjoying the full blaze of the westing sun. Leonard, his canvas garments wet with perspiration, his legs aching, leaned against the back of the bench and wondered why he wanted to play football!

Presently he forgot his discomforts in watching the performance of a squad of fellows who were trotting through a signal drill. Last year's regulars these, he supposed; big, heavy chaps, most of them; fellows whose average age was possibly eighteen, or perhaps more. The quarterback, unlike most of the quarters Leonard had had acquaintance with, was a rather large and weighty youth with light hair and a longish face. His name, explained Leonard's left-hand neighbor on the bench, was Carpenter. He had played on the second team last year and was very likely to prove first-choice man this fall. He was, the informant added admiringly, a corking punter. Leonard nodded. Secretly he considered Mr. Carpenter much too heavy for a quarterback's job. The day's diversions ended with a slow jog around the edge of the gridiron. Then came showers and a leisurely dressing; only Leonard, since his street clothes were over in Number 12 Haylow, had his shower in the dormitory and was wearily clothing himself in clean underwear and a fresh shirt when the door of the room was unceremoniously opened and he found himself confronted by a youth whose countenance was strangely familiar and whom, his reason told him, was Eldred Chichester Staples, his poetic roommate. Considering it later, Leonard wondered why he had not been more surprised when recognition came. All he said was: "Well, did you get rid of the whole seventeen?"

CHAPTER IV
LEONARD GETS PROMOTION

Eldred Chichester Staples appeared to be no more surprised than Leonard. He closed the door, with the deftness born of long practice, with his left foot, sailed his cap to his bed and nodded, thrusting hands into the pockets of his knickers.

"The whole seventeen," he answered dejectedly. "Couldn't you tell it by a glance at my emaciated frame?"

Leonard shook his head. "You look to me just hungry," he said.

"Slim" Staples chuckled and reposed himself in a chair, thrusting his long legs forward and clasping lean, brown hands across his equator. "Your name must be Grant," he remarked. "Where from, stranger?"

"Loring Point, Delaware."

"We're neighbors then. My home's in New Hampshire. Concord's the town."

"Isn't that where the embattled farmers stood and—and fired—er—"

"The shot that was heard around the world? No, General, you've got the dope all wrong. That was another Concord. There aren't any farmers in my town. Come to think of it, wasn't it Lexington, Massachusetts, where the farmers took pot-shots at the Britishers? Well, never mind. I understand that the affair was settled quite amicably some time since. Glad to be here, General?"

"I think so. Thanks for the promotion, though. I'm usually just 'Len.'"

"Oh, that's all right. No trouble to promote you. What does 'Len' stand for?"

"Leonard."

"Swell name. You've got the edge on the other Grant. Ulysses sounds like something out of the soda fountain. Well, I hope we'll hit it off all right. I'm an easy-going sort, General; never much of a scrapper and hate to argue. Last year, over in Borden, I roomed with

21

a chap named Endicott. Dick was the original arguer. He could start with no take-off at all and argue longer, harder and faster than any one outside a court of law. I was a great trial to him, I suspect. If he said Ralph Waldo Emerson wrote 'The Merchant of Venice' I just said 'Sure, Mike' and let it go at that. Arguing was meat and drink to that fellow."

"And what became of him? I mean, why aren't you—"

"Together this year? He didn't come back. You see, he spent so much time in what you might call controversy that he didn't get leisure for studying. So last June faculty told him that he'd failed to pass and that if he came back he'd have about a million conditions to work off. He did his best to argue himself square, but faculty beat him out. After all, there was only one of him and a dozen or so faculty, and it wasn't a fair contest. At that, I understand they won by a very slight margin!"

"Hard luck," laughed Leonard. "I dare say he was a star member of the debating club, if there is one here."

"There is, but Dick never joined. He said they were amateurs. What do you say to supper? Oh, by the way, you were out for football, weren't you? What's your line?"

"I've played guard mostly."

"Guard, eh?" Slim looked him over appraisingly. "Sort of light, aren't you?"

"I guess so," allowed Leonard. "Of course, I don't expect to make the first; that is, this year."

Slim grinned wickedly. "No, but you'll be fit to tie if you don't. Take me now. Last year I was on the second. Left end. I'm only a soph, and sophs on the big team are as scarce as hen's teeth. So, of course, I haven't the ghost of a show and absolutely no hope of making it. But if I don't there's going to be a heap of trouble around here!"

"Well, I suppose I have a sneaking hope," acknowledged Leonard, smiling.

"Sure. Might as well be honest with yourself. As for playing guard, well, if you got hold of a suit about three sizes too large for you, stuffed it out with cotton-batting and put heel-lifts in your shoes you might stand a show. Or you might if it wasn't for this fellow Renneker. I dare say you've heard about him? He's ab-so-lutively sure of one guard position or the other. And then there's Smedley and Squibbs and Raleigh and Stimson and two-three more maybe If I were you, General, I'd switch to end or quarter."

"Oh, I wouldn't want to elbow you out," laughed Leonard.

"That's right." Slim grinned. "Try quarter then. We've got only two in sight so far."

Leonard shook his head. "Guard's my job," he said. "I'll plug along at it. I might get on the second, I dare say. And next year— The trouble is, I can't seem to grow much, Staples!"

"Better call me 'Slim.' Everybody else does. Well, you know your own business best. Only, if you tell Johnny that you belong to the Guard's Union and that the rules won't allow you to play anything else, why, I'm awfully afraid that the only thing you'll get to guard will be the bench! Let's go to chow."

At the door of the dining hall they parted, for Slim's table was not Leonard's. "But," said the former, "I guess we can fix that to-morrow. There are a couple of guys at our table that don't fit very well. I'll arrange with one of them to switch. Care to go over to Mac's this evening? Being a newcomer, you're sort of expected to. They'll be mostly freshies, but we don't have to stay long. I'll pick you up at the room about eight."

Under Slim's guidance Leonard went across to the Principal's house at a little after the appointed hour and took his place in the line that led through the front portal and past where Doctor McPherson and Mrs. McPherson were receiving. Slim introduced the stranger and then hustled him away into the library. "Might as well do it all up brown," he observed sotto voce. "Met any of the animals yet?"

"Animals?" repeated Leonard vaguely.

"Faculty," explained Slim. "All right. We'll find most of 'em in here. They can see the dining room from here, you'll observe, and so they sort of stand around, ready to rush the minute the flag goes down. Not so many here yet. Try to look serious and intellectual; they like it. Mr. Screven, I want you to meet my friend Grant. General, this is Mr. Screven. And Mr. Metcalf. Mr. Metcalf wrote the French and Spanish languages, General."

"If I had, Staples, I'd have written them more simply, so you could learn them," replied the instructor with a twinkle.

"*Touche!*" murmured Slim. "Honest, though, I wasn't so rotten, was I, sir?"

"You might have been much worse, Staples. Don't ask me to say more."

"Well, I'll make a real hit with you this year, sir. They say Sophomore French is a cinch."

"I trust you'll find it so," replied Mr. Metcalf genially. "Where is your home, Mr. Grant?"

Presently Slim's hand tugged him away to meet Mr. Tarbot and Mr. Kincaid and Mr. Peghorn, by which time Leonard couldn't remember which was which, although Slim's running comment, en route from one to another, was designed to aid his friend's memory. "Peghorn's physics," appraised Slim. "You won't have him, not this year. He's a bit deaf. Left ear's the best one. Don't let him nail you or he'll talk you to death. Here we are."

There were others later, but Leonard obtained sustenance before meeting them, for Slim so skillfully maneuvered that when the dining room doors were thrown open only a mere half-dozen guests beat him to the table. To the credit of the faculty be it said that Mr. Kincaid only lost first place by a nose. The refreshments were satisfactory if not elaborate and Slim worked swiftly and methodically, and presently, their plates well piled with sandwiches, cake and ice-cream, the two retired to a corner. The entering class was large that fall and, since not a few of the other classes were well represented, the Doctor's modest residence was crowded. Slim observed pessimistically that he had never seen a sorrier looking lot of freshies.

"How about last year?" asked Leonard innocently.

"The entering class last year," replied Slim with dignity, "was remarkably intelligent and—um—prepossessing. Every one spoke of it. Even members of the class themselves noticed it. Want another slice of cake?"

Leonard rather pitied some of the new boys. They looked so timid and unhappy, he thought. Most of them had no acquaintances as yet, and although the faculty members and some of the older fellows worked hard to put them at their ease they continued looking like lost souls. Even ice-cream and cake failed to banish their embarrassment. The Principal's wife, good soul, haled them from dark corners and talked to them brightly and cheerfully while she thrust plates of food into their numbed hands, but so soon as her back was turned they fled nervously to cover again, frequently losing portions of their refreshments on the way. Reflecting that even he might do some small part to lighten the burden of gloom that oppressed them, he broached the subject to Slim when that youth had returned with another generous wedge of cake. But Slim shook his head.

"I wouldn't," he said. "Honestly, General, they're a lot happier left alone. I'm supposed to be on the welcome committee myself, but I'm not working at it much. Fact is, those poor fish had a lot rather you didn't take any notice of them. They just get red in the face and fall over their feet if you speak to 'em. I know, for I was one myself last year!"

"Somehow," mused Leonard, "I can't imagine it."

"Can't you now?" Slim chuckled. "I want you to know that the shrinking violet hasn't a thing on me. Chuck your plate somewhere and let's beat it. There's no hope of seconds!"

Back in Number 12 Haylow they changed to pajamas and lolled by the window, through which a fair imitation of a cooling breeze occasionally wandered, and proceeded to get acquainted. It wasn't hard. By ten o'clock, when the light went out, they were firm friends and tried.

The business of settling down consumed several days, and as the Fall Term at Alton Academy began on a Thursday it was Monday before Leonard really found himself. Slim was of great assistance to him in the operation and saved him many false moves and unnecessary steps. As both boys were in the same class Leonard had only to copy Slim's schedule and, during the first day, follow Slim dutifully from one recitation room to another, at the end of each trip renewing Wednesday evening's acquaintance with one or another of the faculty members, though at a distance. In various other matters Slim was invaluable. Thursday evening Leonard took his place at Slim's table and so enlarged his circle of speaking acquaintances by eight. Several of the occupants of the board Leonard recognized as football candidates. There was, for instance, Wells, universally known as "Billy," heir apparent to the position of left tackle, and Joe Greenwood, who might fairly be called heir presumptive to the fullback position, only one Ray Goodwin thus far showing a better right. There was, also, Leo Falls, who, like Leonard, was a candidate for guard. Thus, five out of the ten were football players, a fact which not only made for camaraderie, but provided a never-failing subject for conversation. Of the others at the table, two were freshmen, likeable youngsters, Leonard thought; one was a sober-faced senior named Barton, and the other two were juniors who, being the sole representatives of their class there, were banded together in an offensive and defensive alliance that, in spite of its lack of numbers, was well able to hold its own when the question of class supremacy was debated. On the whole, they were a jolly set, and Leonard was thankful to Slim for securing him admission to them; even though, as Slim reminded him, several of them would be yanked off to the training table not later than next week.

What the others thought of Leonard the latter didn't know, but they seemed to take to him readily. Perhaps the fact that he was sponsored by Slim had something to do with it, for Slim, as Leonard soon noted, was a favorite, not only at his table but throughout the school in general. (The fact that Slim was President of the Sophomore Class was something that Leonard didn't learn until he had been rooming with the former for nearly three weeks; and then it wasn't Slim who divulged it.) I don't mean to convey the idea that Leonard was unduly exercised about the impression he made on his new friends, but no fellow can help wanting to be liked or speculate somewhat about what others think of him. After a few days, though, he became quite satisfied. By that time no one at the board was any longer calling him Grant. He was "General." Slim's nickname had struck the popular fancy and gave every sign of sticking throughout Leonard's stay at school.

There wasn't anything especially striking about the newcomer, unless, perhaps, it was a certain wholesomeness; which Slim, had he ever been required to tell what had drawn him to his new chum, would have mentioned first. Leonard was of average height, breadth and weight. He had good enough features, but no one would ever have thought to call him handsome. His hair was of an ordinary shade of brown, straight and inclined to be unruly around the ears and neck; his eyes were brown, too, though a shade or two darker; perhaps his eyes were his best feature, if there was a best, for they did have a sort of faculty for lighting up when he became interested or deeply amused; his nose was straight as far as it went, but it stopped a trifle too soon to satisfy the demands of the artist; his mouth was just like any other mouth, I suppose; that is, like any other normal mouth; and he had a chin that went well with his somewhat square jaw, with a scarcely noticeable elevation in the middle of it that Slim referred to as an inverted dimple. Just a normal, healthy youngster of sixteen, was Leonard—sixteen verging closely on seventeen—rather better developed muscularly than the average boy of his years, perhaps, but with nothing about him to demand a second glance; or certainly not a third. He didn't dress particularly well, for his folks weren't over-supplied with wealth, but he managed to make the best of a limited wardrobe and always looked particularly clean. He was inclined to be earnest at whatever he set out to do, but he liked to laugh and did it frequently, and did it in a funny gurgling way that caused others to laugh with him— and at him.

He might have made his way into the Junior Class at Alton had he tutored hard the previous summer, but as he had not known he was going there until a fortnight before, that wasn't possible. His presence at the academy was the unforeseen result of having spent the summer with his Uncle Emory. Uncle Emory, his mother's brother, lived up in Pennsylvania and for many years had displayed no interest in the doings of his relatives. The idea of visiting Uncle Emory and working for his board had come to Leonard after Tim

Walsh, football coach at the high school, had mentioned farm work as one of the short paths to physical development. Rather to the surprise of the rest of the family, Uncle Emory's reply to Leonard's suggestion had been almost cordial. Uncle Emory had proved much less of the bear than the boy had anticipated and before long the two were very good friends. By the terms of the agreement, Leonard was to receive board and lodging and seventy-five cents a day in return for his services. What he did receive, when the time for leaving the farm arrived, was ninety-three dollars, being wages due him, and a bonus of one hundred.

"And now," asked Uncle Emory, "what are you doing to do with it?"

Leonard didn't know. He was far too surprised to make plans on such short notice.

"Well," continued Uncle Emory, "why don't you find yourself a good school that don't ask too much money and fit yourself for college? I ain't claiming that your father's made a big success as a lawyer, but you might, and I sort of think it's in your blood. You show me that you mean business, Len, and I'll sort of look out for you, leastways till you're through school."

So that is the way it had happened, suddenly and unexpectedly and gorgeously. The hundred and ninety-three dollars, less Leonard's expenses home, hadn't been enough to see him through the year at Alton, but his father had found the balance that was needed without much difficulty, and here he was. He knew that this year was provided for and knew that, if he satisfied Uncle Emory of his earnestness, there would be two more years to follow. Also, a fact that had not escaped Leonard, there were scholarship funds to be had if one worked hard enough. He had already set his mind on winning one of the five available to Sophomore Class members. As to the Law as a profession, Leonard hadn't yet made up his mind. Certainly his father had made no fortune from it, but, on the other hand, there were men right in Loring Point who had prospered exceedingly thereby. But that decision could wait. Meanwhile he meant to study hard, win a scholarship and make good in the eyes of Uncle Emory. And he meant to play as hard as he worked, which was an exceedingly good plan, and hadn't yet discerned any very good reason for not doing that on the Alton Academy Football Team!

CHAPTER V
THE BOY ON THE PORCH

He liked the school immensely and the fellows in it. And he liked the town, with its tree-shaded streets and comfortable old white houses. A row of the latter faced the Academy from across the asphalt thoroughfare below the sloping campus, home-like residences set in turf and gardens, guarded by huge elms and maples. Beyond them began, a block further east, the stores. One could get nearly anything he wanted in the two short blocks of West street, without journeying closer to the center of town. In school parlance this shopping district was known as Bagdad. Further away one found moving picture houses in variety. Northward at some distance lay the river, and under certain not too painful restrictions one might enjoy boating and canoeing. On Sunday Alton rang with the peeling of church bells and Bagdad was empty of life save, perhaps, for a shrill-voiced purveyor of newspapers from whom one could obtain for a dime an eight-section New York paper with which to litter the floor after the return from church. On that first Sunday Slim acted as guide and Leonard learned what lay around and about. They penetrated to the sidewalk-littered foreign quarter beyond the railroad, where Slim tried modern Greek on a snappily-attired gentleman who to-morrow would be presiding over a hat cleaning emporium. The result was not especially favorable. Either Slim's knowledge of Greek was too limited or, as he explained it, the other chap didn't know his own language. Then they wandered southward, to the Hill, and viewed the ornate mansions of the newly rich. Here were displayed tapestry brick and terra cotta, creamy limestone and colorful tile, pergolas and stained glass, smooth lawns and concrete walks, immaculate hedges and dignified shrubs. Being a newer part of town, the trees along the streets were small and threw little shade on the sun-heated pavement, and this, combined with the fact that to reach the Hill one had of necessity to negotiate a grade, left the boys rather out of breath and somewhat too warm for comfort. On the whole, Leonard liked the older part of Alton much better, and confided the fact to his companion.

"So do I," agreed Slim. "Of course these places up here have a lot of things the old houses lack; like tennis courts and garages and sleeping porches; but there's an old white house on River street, just around the corner from Academy, that hits me about right. I'll show it to you some time. I guess it's about a hundred years old; more, likely; but, gee, it's a corking old place. When I have a house of my own, General, none of these young city halls or Carnegie libraries for mine! I want a place that looks as if some one lived in it. Take a squint at that chocolate brick arrangement over there. Can you imagine any one being really comfortable in it? Why, if I lived there I'd be always looking for a bell-hop to spring out on me and grab whatever I had and push me over to the register so I could sign my name and get a key. That's a fine, big porch, but I'll bet you wouldn't ever think of sitting out there on a summer evening in your shirt sleeves and sprinkling water on that trained mulberry tree!"

"I don't believe," laughed Leonard, "that they put anything as common as water on that cute thing. They probably have a Mulberry Tree Tonic or something like that they bathe it in. Say, there is some one on the porch, just the same, and it looks to me as if he was waving to us."

"Why, that's Johnny McGrath!" said Slim. "Hello, Johnny! That where you live?"

"Sure. Come on over!"

Slim looked inquiringly at Leonard. "Want to go?" he asked in low tones. "Johnny's a good sort."

Leonard nodded, if without enthusiasm, and Slim led the way across the ribbon of hot asphalt and up the three stone steps that led, by the invariable concrete path, to the wide porch. A boy of about Leonard's age stood awaiting them at the top of the steps, a round-faced chap with a nose liberally adorned with freckles and undeniably tip-tilted. He wore white flannel trousers and a gray flannel coat, and there was a liberal expanse of gray silk socks exposed above the white shoes.

"Want you to meet my friend Grant," said Slim, climbing the wide steps. "General, this is Johnny McGrath, the only Sinn Feiner in school. What you been doing to-day, Johnny? Making bombs?"

31

Johnny smiled widely and good-humoredly. "You're the only bum I've seen so far," he replied. "Come up and cool off."

"That's a rotten pun," protested Slim, accepting the invitation to sit down in a comfortable wicker chair. "Say, Johnny, there must be money in Sinn Feining." He looked approvingly about the big porch with its tables and chairs, magazines and flowering plants. "Is this your real home, or do you just hire this for Sundays?"

"We've been living here going on three years," answered Johnny. "Ever since dad made his pile." He turned to Leonard and indulged in a truly Irish wink of one very blue eye. "Slim thinks he gets my goat," he explained, "but he doesn't. Sure, I know this is a bit of a change from The Flats."

"The Flats?" repeated Leonard questioningly.

"That's what they call it over beyond the Carpet Mills," explained Johnny. "Shanty Town, you know; Goatville; see?"

"Oh, yes! I don't believe I've been there yet."

"Well, it isn't much to look at," laughed Johnny. "We lived there until about three years ago. We weren't as poor as most of them, but there were six of us in five rooms, Grant. Then dad made his pile and we bought this place." Johnny looked about him not altogether approvingly and shook his head. "It's fine enough, all right, but, say, fellows, it's awfully—what's the word I seen—saw the other day? Stodgy, that's it! I guess it's going to take us another three years to get used to it."

"He misses having the pig in the parlor," observed Slim gravely to Leonard. The latter looked toward Johnny McGrath anxiously, but Johnny only grinned.

"'Twas never that bad with us," he replied, "but I mind the day the Cleary's nanny-goat walked in the kitchen and ate up half of dad's nightshirt, and mother near killed him with a flat-iron!"

"Why did she want to kill your father with a flat-iron?" asked Slim mildly.

"The goat, I said."

"You did not, Johnny. You told us it was a nanny-goat and said your mother nearly killed 'him.' If that doesn't mean your father—"

"Well, anyway, I had to lick Terry Cleary before there was peace between us again," laughed Johnny. Then his face sobered. "Sure, up here on the Hill," he added, "you couldn't find a scrap if you was dying!"

The others had to laugh, Slim ejaculating between guffaws: "Johnny, you'll be the death of me yet!" Johnny's blue eyes were twinkling again and his broad Irish mouth smiling.

"It's mighty queer," he went on, "how grand some of these neighbors of ours are up here. Take the Paternos crowd next door here. Sure, six years ago that old Dago was still selling bananas from a wagon, and to-day—wow!—the only wagon he rides in is a limousine. And once, soon after we moved in, mother was in the back yard seeing the maid hung the clothes right, or something, and there was Mrs. Paternos' black head stuck out of an upstairs window, and thinking to be neighborly, mind you, mother says to her, 'Good morning, ma'am,' or something like that, and the old Eye-talian puts her nose in the air and slams down the windy—window, I mean!"

"You've got to learn, Johnny," explained Slim, "that you can't become an aristocrat, even in this free country of ours, in less than five years. That gives you about two to go, son. Be patient."

"Patient my eye," responded Johnny serenely. "It'll take more than five years to make aristocrats of the McGraths, for they're not wanting it. Just the same, Slim, it makes me sick, the way some folks put on side just because they've been out of the tenements a few years. I guess the lot of us, and I'm meaning you, too, couldn't go very many years back before we'd be finding bananas or lead pipe or something ple-bee-an like that hanging on the old family tree!"

"Speak for yourself," answered Slim with much dignity. "Or speak for the General here. As for the Stapleses, Johnny, I'd have you know that we're descended from Jeremy Staples, who owned the first inn in Concord, New Hampshire, and who himself served a glass of grog to General George Washington!"

"That would be a long time ago," said Johnny.

"It would; which is why we can boast of it. If it happened last year we'd be disclaiming any relationship to the old reprobate."

"McGrath's right," said Leonard, smiling but thoughtful. "We're all descended from trade or something worse. I know a fellow back home whose several-times-great grandfather was a pirate with Stede Bonnet, and his folks are as proud of it as anything. If it isn't impertinent, McGrath, how did your father make his money?"

"In the War, like so many others. He was a plumber, you see. He'd gone into business for himself a few years before and was doing pretty well. Joe—that's my oldest brother—was with him. Well, then the War came and Joe read in the paper where they were going to build a big cantonment for the soldiers over in Jersey. 'Why not try to get the job to put in some of the plumbing?' says he. 'Sure, we haven't a chance,' says my dad. ''Twill be the big fellows as will get that work.' But Joe got a copy of the specifications, or whatever they're called, and set down and figured, and finally persuaded the Old Man to take a chance. So they did, and some surprised they were when they were awarded the contract! Dad said it was too big for them and they'd have to give some of it to another, but Joe wouldn't stand for that. He had a hard time getting money for the bond, or whatever it was the Government wanted, but he did it finally, and they did the job and did it honestly. Their figures were away under the estimate of the other firms, but in spite of that they made themselves rich. Now I say why isn't dad as much of a gentleman as old Pete Paternos? Sure lead pipe's as clean as rotten bananas!"

"That's just the point," replied Slim. "The rotten bananas are old and the lead pipe's new. Give the lead pipe another two years, Johnny, and you can slap Paternos on the back and get away with it."

"I'm more likely to slap him on the head with a crow-bar," grumbled Johnny. Then: "Say, fellows, want some lemonade?"

"Not for worlds," answered Slim promptly. "Where is it?"

"I'll have Dora make a pitcher in a shake of a lamb's tail," said Johnny eagerly, as he disappeared. Slim smiled over at Leonard and Leonard smiled back. Then the latter exclaimed protestingly:

"Just the same, he's a mighty decent sort, Slim!"

"Of course he is," agreed the other calmly. "I told you that across the street. Johnny's all right."

"Well, then, aren't you—aren't you afraid of hurting his feelings? Talking to him the way you do, I mean."

"Not a bit. Johnny knows me, and he knows that what I say is for the good of his soul. We aristocrats, General, have got to make the hoi polloi understand that they can't shove into our sacred circle off-hand. They've got to train for it, old man; work up; go through an initiation."

Leonard observed Slim in puzzlement and doubt.

"Why," Slim went on soberly, "what do you suppose old Jeremy Staples would say if he could see me now hob-nobbing with the son of a plumber? The poor old rascal would turn over in his grave, General. Bet you he'd turn over twice!"

"Oh," said Leonard, "I thought you meant it!"

"Who says I don't? Ah, that sounds mighty cheerful, Johnny! Sure you didn't put any arsenic in it? My folks are English on my uncle's side!"

"I'd not waste good arsenic on the likes of you," answered Johnny, pouring from a frosted glass pitcher. Followed several moments of deeply appreciative silence during which visitors and host applied themselves to the straws that emerged from the glasses. Then Slim sighed rapturously and held his glass out for more.

"It may be poisoned, Johnny," he said, "but I'll take a chance."

"Are you at Alton?" Leonard asked presently of his host.

"Didn't I tell you he was?" asked Slim in mild surprise. "He certainly is. Johnny's the one bright spot on the basket ball team. You'll never know the poetry of motion, General, until you've seen him toss a back-hander into the hoop. The only trouble with him is that, true to his race, he always mistakes a basket ball game for the Battle of the Boyne. At least, I think I mean the Boyne. Do I, Johnny?"

"Maybe. I wasn't there. Anyhow, you're giving Grant here a wrong idea of me entirely. I'm the most peaceable lad on the team, Slim Staples, and you know it."

"I know nothing of the sort," protested Slim stoutly. "All I do know is that whenever you're playing the casualties are twice as heavy as when you're not. Oh, I know you have a foxy way of handing out the wallops, and that the referee seldom catches you at it, but facts are facts, Johnny, and I'm nothing if not factotum."

"You're nothing if not insulting," corrected Johnny. "Why does he call you 'General?'" he continued of Leonard.

"Why, he hit on that—" Leonard began.

"Is it possible you never heard of General Grant?" demanded Slim incredulously.

"Oh, that's it? Well," as Slim stood up to go and Leonard followed his example, "I'm pleased to have met you. Come again, won't you? I'll not be asking Slim, for he's too insulting."

"Oh, now that I know where you live and what good lemonade you keep on draught, I'll come frequently," said Slim kindly. "Maybe we might drop around next Sunday afternoon about this time, or a little before. You'd better make it a point to have plenty of lemons on hand."

"Why, if you come we'll not be without them," Johnny assured him sweetly.

"Fine! And now, before we go, may we see the pig, Johnny?"

"Sure," replied the other, relapsing into a rich brogue, "it's sorry I am, Slim my darlint, but the pig do be havin' his afthernoon nap in the panthry, and he'd be that angry if I was wakin' him!"

Going back down the slope of Melrose Avenue Leonard remarked: "He said there were six of them, Slim. Are there other brothers beside the Joe he spoke of?"

"There were," answered Slim. "There's one other now, a little chap about twelve. I don't know his name."

"What happened to the other brother?"

"Killed in the War," replied Slim briefly.

"Oh!"

"There was a citation," added Slim. "Johnny says it's framed and hanging over his mother's bed. It's a lucky thing for the country, General, that it doesn't have to look up a fellow's pedigree before it can let him fight; what?"

CHAPTER VI
THE SEASON BEGINS

In spite of Slim's predictions, Leonard's calm announcement to Manager Tenney that he was a candidate for guard on the football team occasioned no evident surprise. Considering that within forty-eight hours Tenney had registered the name of a fat and pudgy junior whose consuming ambition was to play quarterback and had listened to the calm assurance of a lathe-like youth that he would be satisfied with nothing save the position of center, the manager's absence of emotion was not surprising. Anyhow, Leonard was relieved to find that he was not to meet opposition at the outset, and took his place in Squad C quite satisfied. Football practice at Alton Academy differed from the same occupation at Loring Point High School in at least two essentials, he decided. It was more systematic and it was a whole lot more earnest. There was little lost motion during the hour and a half that the candidates occupied the field. You didn't stand around waiting for the coach to remember your existence and think up a new torture, nor, when the coach was present, did you spend precious minutes in banter. From the moment of the first "Let's go!" to the final "That's all, fellows!" you had something to do and did it hard, impressed every instant with the importance of the task set you. Of course, practice was less amusing, less fun here at Alton. There was no social side to the gathering. Even after a week of practice Leonard knew almost none of the fellows he worked with. He did know the names of many, and he had a "Hello" acquaintance with a half-dozen, but there was no time for the social amenities.

He had been put down as a lineman and spent at least a half-hour daily being instructed in the duties of blocking and charging. Always there was another half-hour for each squad with the tackling dummies, of which headless opponents there were two. Generally the balance of the period was occupied in learning to handle the ball and in running through a few simple formation plays. In these Leonard was played anywhere that the assistant coach, usually acting as quarter, fancied. Generally he was a guard or a tackle, now on this side and now on that, but on two occasions he found himself

38

cast for a backfield rôle and trotted up and down the field as a half. On Tuesday afternoon the first and second squads held the first scrimmage, and by Thursday Coach Cade had put together a tentative eleven to meet Alton High School on Saturday. No one was surprised to see Gordon Renneker occupying the position of right guard, for Renneker's fame had already spread throughout the school.

That first engagement was played under a hot sun and with the temperature hovering around seventy-two when High School kicked off. Naturally enough, as an exhibition of scientific football it left much to be desired. High School showed lack of condition and her players were to be seen stretched on their backs whenever time was called. Alton appeared of somewhat sterner stuff, but there was no doubt that half-time came as a welcome interruption even to her. "Johnny" Cade started Gurley and Emerson at ends, Butler and Wilde at tackles, Stimson and Renneker at guards and Garrick at center. The backfield consisted of Carpenter, Goodwin, Kendall and Greenwood. But this line-up didn't persist long. Even by the end of the first quarter "Red" Reilly was at right half and Wells was at right tackle. During the remainder of the game changes were frequent until, near the end of the final period, second- and third-string players made up the team. Coach Cade tried out much unknown material that afternoon, and it seemed to Leonard that he was the only candidate who hadn't been given a chance. As a matter of fact, though, there were some twenty others in like case, for the squad had not yet been cut. It was when Alton was presenting her weakest line-up that High School cut loose with her second bombardment of overhead shots—the first essay, in the second quarter, had netted her little enough—and secured her lone touchdown. She failed to add a goal since her line didn't hold long enough for her kicker to get the ball away. The final score of the slow and ragged contest was 23 to 6. Talking it over afterwards in the comparative coolness of Number 12 Haylow, Slim was pessimistic. Perhaps the fact that his own efforts during approximately half of the forty minutes of actual play had not been brilliantly successful colored his mood.

There was another half-hour for each squad with the tackling
dummies

"We've got plenty of material," pronounced Slim, elevating his
scantily-clad legs to the window-sill, "and I guess it's average good,
but it's going to take us a long time to get going this year. You can
see that with half an eye. Look at the army of queers that Johnny

tried out this afternoon. That's what slows up development, General. Now, last year we had the makings of a team right at the start. Only three or four first-string lads, I think, but a perfect gang of experienced substitutes, to say nothing of second team fellows. Result was that we started off with a bang and kept going. You bet High School didn't do any scoring last season!"

"But," objected Leonard, "weren't you telling me the other day that the team had an awful slump about the middle of the season, and—"

"Oh, well, that had nothing to do with the start. Two or three things accounted for that. What I'm getting at is just this. It's mighty poor policy to spend the first two weeks of a football season finding out that more than half of your material's no good to you. If I ever coach a team there'll be no mob under my feet after the first three or four days. Thirty men'll be all I'll want. If I can't build a team out of them, all right. I get out."

"Glad that rule doesn't hold good now," said Leonard. "If it did I'd be out of it already."

"Well, I don't know. No, you wouldn't either! That's what I'm getting at. You can play football. You've done it for two years. You've had experience. All right. But look at the run of the small fry that—that's infesting the field so you have to watch your step to keep from tramping on 'em. Why, suffering cats, most of 'em won't be ready to play football for two years yet! There are chaps out there who couldn't stop a ball with their heads! The ball would knock 'em right over. Well, Johnny gives each of 'em the once-over, and it takes time. He knows they aren't going to show anything. It's just this silly policy of giving every one a chance to make good. That's why you're sitting on the bench and a bunch of scrawny little would-be's are letting High School shove over a score on us."

"You may be right," answered Leonard, "but it seems to me that it's only by giving every one a chance to show what he's good for that you can be sure of not overlooking something. I've seen more than once a fellow who didn't look like anything at all at the start of the season turn into something good later on."

"Sure, that happens now and then, but what of it? If the fellow really has ability he keeps on playing. He goes to the scrubs or one of the class teams. If he makes good there he mighty soon finds himself yanked back to the first. And the coach hasn't wasted a week or two trying to find out about him."

"Well, I guess I'm—I'm conservative, or something," laughed Leonard, "for I sort of like a team that starts slow and gets up its speed gradually. I know that back home our coach used to point us for our big game, the last one, and all the other games were taken as they came, more or less. Of course, when we played Delaware Polytechnic we smoothed out a bit and learned two or three new plays just beforehand, but we didn't go out of our way much even for her."

"Oh, that's all right, General. I don't want to see any team hit its stride too early. Safe and slow is my motto, too, but that doesn't mean you've got to get started a fortnight after school opens. Look here, I'll bet you that next Saturday Johnny won't be any nearer settled on the team's make-up than he was to-day. Well, of course, he'll know about some positions, but he'll still be experimenting. Rus Emerson's the same sort he is, too; has an ingrown conscience or—or sense of responsibility toward others. If Rus had his way any fellow who could borrow a pair of football pants could have a week's try-out!"

"Who plays us next Saturday?" asked Leonard.

"Lorimer Academy. They're a nice crowd of chaps, and they don't give us much trouble. Last year, though, they did sort of throw a scare into us. We got three scores to their two. It was right after that we played a tie game with Hillsport and went into a jolly slump. Say, that guy Renneker didn't show up so mighty wonderful to-day, did you think?"

"N-no, he looked a bit slow to me. But I guess he hasn't got used to the place yet. Either that or he was sort of saving himself."

"Saving himself for what?" demanded Slim.

"Search me." Leonard smiled. "Maybe he thought there wasn't much use working too hard against a weak team like Alton High."

Slim shook his head, looking incredulous. "All I know is that the short time we were in together he was generally 'on the outside looking in.' Rather gives me the impression of being a poser. Still, to-day wasn't much of a test; and he's pretty big and perhaps the heat stalled him some. Hope he pans out big, for we sure need a corking good guard. Smedley's a pippin, and Raleigh isn't too bad, but we need another. To look at Renneker you'd expect him to be a hustler, but he didn't show it to-day. He was outside most of the plays when I saw him. Not like Jim Newton. Jim's always in the middle of it. For a center, Jim's a live wire. Doesn't matter much where the play comes in the line; Jim's always sitting on the enemy's head when the dust clears away! Say, I wish you'd switch your game, General, and try for tackle or something, something you'd have a show at."

"But you just said," answered the other demurely, "that the team needed another good guard."

Slim grinned and shook his head. "All right, son, but I'd like to see you on the team. That's all."

"Think one of us ought to get on, eh?"

"Huh? Oh, well, there's something in that, too. I'm not very sure of a place, and that's no jolly quip. Gurley's a good end, worse luck! And there's Kerrison, too. But I'll give them a fight for it. They'll know they've been working if they beat me out, General! Let's go and see what they're giving us for supper."

Leonard met the captain that evening for the first time. Met him socially, that is to say, Russell Emerson and Billy Wells overtook Leonard and Slim on their way to the movies. Wells was one of those Leonard already had a speaking acquaintance with, but Emerson had thus far remained outside his orbit. Continuing the journey, Leonard fell to Billy Wells and Rus and Slim walked ahead, but coming home they paired differently and Leonard found himself conversing with the captain, at first somewhat embarrassedly. But the football captain was easy to know, as the saying is, and Leonard soon forgot his diffidence. Of course, football formed some of the conversation, but Leonard sensed relief on the other's part when the subject changed to the pictures they had just witnessed. After that they talked of other things; the school, and Leonard's home in Rhode Island—Rus, it seemed, had never been farther south than he was now—, and the faculty and some of the fellows. The captain seemed to take it for granted that his companion was familiar with the names he mentioned, although as a fact most of them were new to Leonard. Mention of "Jake," the trainer, introduced a laughable story about Jake and a track team candidate, in which Rus tried to imitate Jake's brogue. That reminded Leonard of Johnny McGrath, and he asked Rus if he knew him.

"Yes, I've met him several times," was the answer. "I've been trying to get him to try football. He's a very good basket ball player and I've a strong hunch that he'd make a corking half. But his folks, his mother especially, I believe, object. He had a brother killed in the War, and his mother is dead set against taking chances with another of them. Too bad, too, for he's a fast, scrappy fellow. The good-natured kind, you know. Plays hard and keeps his temper every minute. There's a lot in keeping your temper, Grant."

"But I've heard of teams being 'fighting mad' and doing big things."

"Yes, the phrase is common enough, but 'fighting earnest' would be better. Just as soon as a fellow gets really mad he loses his grip more or less. He makes mistakes of judgment, begins to play 'on his own.' If he gets angry enough he stops being any use to the team. Of course there are chaps now and then who can work themselves up to a sort of fighting fury and play great football, but I suspect that those chaps aren't really quite as wild as they let on. There's Billy back there. He almost froths at the mouth and insults the whole team he's playing against, but he never loses anything more than his tongue, I guess. The old bean keeps right on functioning as per usual. Billy doesn't begin to warm up until his opponent double-crosses him or some one hands him a wallop! By the way, Grant, you're on the squad, aren't you? Seems to me I've seen you out at the field."

"Yes," Leonard assented, "I'm trying."

"Good! What position?"

"Guard," answered Leonard stoutly.

"Sure?"

"I beg pardon?"

Emerson smiled. "I mean, are you certain that's the position you want? You look a little light for guard."

"I suppose I am," said Leonard ruefully. "I tried hard to grow last summer, but I didn't succeed very well. Our coach back home insists that I ought to play guard and so I'm sticking to it. Probably I won't have much of a show this year, though."

"Have you been in a scrimmage yet?"

"No, I haven't. I've been on Squad C for a week or so. I've been at guard and tackle, and played back, too. Sort of a utility man."

"Well, if you're on C you haven't done so badly. We'll have to try you in the scrimmage some afternoon. To be honest, though, Grant, you'd have a better chance to get placed at tackle than at guard, for it just happens that we're pretty well fixed for guard material this year. At least, we think so now. We may change our minds later. After all, a fellow who can play guard ought to fit pretty well into the tackle position. I dare say you'd rather do that than not get anywhere."

"I guess so," replied Leonard. Then he laughed. "I suppose I'm sort of stubborn about playing guard, Emerson. I've just had it dinned into me that guard's my game, and I can't seem to take kindly to doing something else. But, as you say, I'd rather play any position at all than none!"

"Why, yes. Besides, you don't have to stick where they put you. I knew a fellow who started here in his second year as half-back on the scrub team, went to the first as end the next year and then played a corking game at center in his senior year. I guess that was an unusual case, but lots of chaps switch from line to backfield and vice versa. Well, here's my hang-out." The captain paused in front of Lykes. "I'm in 16, Grant. Come and see me some time, won't you? Slim knows the way."

Slim and Billy Wells joined them and then the latter and Rus Emerson said good night and went into Lykes. Slim thrust an arm through Leonard's as they continued toward their own dormitory. "Well, what did you and Rus cook up?" he inquired.

"We settled one or two things; such as dropping you and Gurley to the second and putting me in at left end."

"Fine! Anything else?"

"Well, he said that if I didn't like that he'd fix it for me to play tackle. Of course I told him that guard was my game, and he was awfully decent about offering to let Renneker go and putting me in at right guard, but I saw that it would make it a bit awkward for him, and I put my foot down on it at once."

"You would," said Slim admiringly. "You've got a kind heart, General. I'll say that for you. I wish," added Slim feelingly, "I could think of something else to say for you!"

CHAPTER VII
JUST ONE OF THE SUBS

It wasn't until Wednesday of that week that Captain Emerson's quasi-promise bore fruit. Then Coach Cade, consulting his notebook, announced "Lawrence and Grant, tackles." Leonard wasn't quite certain he had heard correctly, but Leo Falls, beside him on the bench, nudged him into action and he cast off his enveloping gray blanket and picked up a helmet.

"Substitutes take the north goal and kick off," directed the coach. "All right, Appel! Hurry it up!"

Leonard trotted out with ten other youths and called to Appel, substitute quarter in charge: "Where do I go?" he asked.

"What are you playing?"

"Tackle."

"Well, for the love of lemons, don't you know your position at kick-off?" asked Appel impatiently. "Get in there between Squibbs and Gurley."

As, however, Lawrence beat him to that location, Leonard disobeyed orders and sandwiched himself in at the left side of the line. Then Garrick kicked off and the scrimmage started. Truth compels me to say that Leonard did not cover himself with glory during the ten minute period allowed him. He tried hard enough, but there *is* a difference between playing guard and playing tackle, and Leonard was much too unfamiliar with the subtleties of a tackle's duties to put up much of a game. Besides, he was faced by two veterans in the persons of Captain Emerson at end and Billy Wells at tackle on the first. Raleigh, who played guard beside him, gave him hurried cues more than once when the play was headed his way, but that didn't always prevent him from being turned in by the truculent Wells while a first team back galloped past for a gain. On offense Leonard did better, but he couldn't think of much to console himself with when the period was over. First had scored twice, once by a touchdown and once by a field-goal, and the subs had never got inside the other's thirty. To add to Leonard's discomfiture, he had plainly heard Appel inquire on one occasion, seemingly of the blue empyrean, and in pained tones, what he had done to be inflicted with a tackle who couldn't stop a toy balloon! About the only thing that Leonard could think of to be thankful for was the fact that Carpenter had selected the right of the sub's line for the attack that had brought the touchdown. It wasn't much, but it was something!

With half a dozen others he was sent off to the showers after the first period, and so he couldn't see that Cash, who took his place in the succeeding period, did scarcely any better. Since Cash, though a newcomer, was a professed tackle, Leonard might have been cheered a trifle by witnessing that youth's performance. As it was, however, it remained for Slim to dispel the gloom to some slight extent. "Why, you poor prune," scoffed Slim later on in Number 12, "you don't need to get hipped about what happened to you. Why, say, if you think you played punk you ought to see some of 'em! Bless your dear soul, sonnie, you were head and shoulders above a lot that get in. I was rather too busy myself to watch how you were getting on very much, but as I didn't hear Appel saying much to you I judge that you did fairly well."

Leonard repeated the quarter's remark about a tackle who couldn't stop a toy balloon, but Slim only chuckled. "If that's all 'Bee' said you must have done mighty well," he answered. "That little hornet has a sting when he wants to use it, believe me, General! And if he'd been really out of patience with you he'd have been all over you!"

"Well, I can't play tackle," said Leonard sadly. "That's one sure thing."

"Oh, piffle! Snap out of it, General. To-morrow, or whenever you get another chance, you'll do a heap better. Anyway, you were on the hard side there, with Billy and Rus against you. Those two tough guys could make any one look sick!"

"I don't believe I'll get another chance," said Leonard.

"Sure, you will. I dare say Johnny'll have you back there to-morrow. Just you forget about being on earth for the sole purpose of playing guard and watch how the tackles handle their jobs. Then you go in and bust things wide open. If Billy gets too gay with you and passes out compliments, tell him where to get off and poke your elbow in his face. Don't let him think you're soft and easy, whatever you do. But, if you'll take my advice, you'll play right tackle next time!"

"N-no," said Leonard, "I guess I'll stick where I was to-day—if I get another chance to."

"You'll get the chance," predicted Slim. "And I don't know but what you're right, at that. You'll learn a heap more and learn it quicker playing opposite Billy than you would against Butler."

Disquieting rumors had reached Alton from Lorimer Academy. The Lorimer team was said to be unusually good this season, and since when only ordinarily good it gave Alton a hard battle, it was considered wise to make a few extra preparations for the next game. The result of this decision was to eliminate scrimmage on Thursday. Instead the first team and substitutes underwent a double dose of signal drill and learned two new plays. Perhaps the plays weren't exactly new; few are any longer; but they were new to Alton, and Coach Cade devoutly hoped that they'd be new to Lorimer! Leonard, trailing his blanket around the sod in the wake of the team, was disappointed, for he had hoped to get another try-out to-day and had earnestly resolved to comport himself so much better than yesterday that Quarterback Appel would ask no more despairing questions of the heavens. But it was not to be. Instead, he was relegated to the rôle of looker-on, he and some twenty others, and so wandered up and down the field behind the workers, supposedly imbibing wisdom as he went. Finally all were dismissed except a handful of kickers and sent back to the gymnasium and showers.

The first cut was announced the next morning, and that afternoon the second team came into being. Leonard was as surprised as relieved to find his name not among the seventeen on the list. He read it three times to make sure. Then he remembered that there would be other cuts coming, and felt less jubilant. There was a long and hard scrimmage that Friday afternoon, but he didn't get into it. However, since the coach had his thoughts centered on the morrow's contest that day, Leonard was not unduly chagrined. It wasn't likely that any fellow who hadn't a chance of being called on to face Lorimer would command Mr. Cade's attention to-day. The new plays didn't go any too well, and some of the older ones went little better. On the whole, there was a general air of dissatisfaction apparent about the field and, later, in the locker room of the gymnasium. Of course, as Slim remarked, walking back to hall with Leonard, beating Lorimer "wasn't anything to get het up about, but, just the same and nevertheless and notwithstanding, it would sort of feel good to hand those lads a wallop!"

"I've got a hunch we'll win," said Leonard comfortably.

"You have, eh? Well, I've got a hunch that we'll have to show more form than we did to-day if we do lick 'em," answered Slim grimly. "No one had any punch this afternoon. I don't blame Johnny for being sore."

"Was he?" asked Leonard, surprised.

"Was he! I'll say he was! Don't you know the symptoms yet?"

Leonard shook his head apologetically. "I guess I don't. He didn't say much, did he?"

"No, he said mighty little. That's his way. When he gets sore he shuts his mouth like a clam. Oh, of course, he talks up to a certain point, but after that—" Slim shook his head. "This afternoon he was so silent it was creepy! I wouldn't be much surprised if there was a fine old shake-up about Monday. Well, we who are about to die salute you!"

Slim drew aside at the entrance to Haylow, his fingers at his forehead, and Leonard passed impressively by.

"I shall always remember you kindly, Slim," he said.

Leonard had been watching the Lorimer game exactly four and one-half minutes the next afternoon when the conviction reached him that the Gray-and-Gold was in for some hard work. It was four and a half minutes after the start of the contest that the Lorimer Academy full-back shot through the left side of the Alton line and, shaking himself free from the secondary defense, plunged on for fourteen yards before he was finally dragged down, landing the pigskin on the home team's thirty-five. Leonard's conviction was accompanied by a premonition of defeat. There was something decidedly awe-inspiring in the smooth efficiency of the invading horde. They were big chaps; big in a rangy way, though, and not merely heavy with flesh; and they moved with speed and precision and a kind of joyous zest that promised trouble for those who should get in their way. According to the stories one heard, the Lorimer team was composed entirely of third and fourth year men, with five of the eleven first-choice players seniors. Leonard could well believe that, for none of the enemy appeared to be less than eighteen years old, while three or four were probably nearer twenty. Opposed to them was a team of much younger players, of whom only three were seniors. Greenwood and Smedley, oldest of all, were but nineteen. Captain Emerson was eighteen. The balance of the players ranged from eighteen down to, in the case of Menge, sixteen. Alton was, also, many pounds lighter, especially in the backfield. Coach Cade might have presented a heavier line-up than he had presented, however. With Newton at center in place of Garrick and Stimson at left guard in place of Smedley the line would have gained several pounds of weight. The backfield likewise might have been improved in the matter of avoirdupois by substituting Goodwin for the diminutive "Cricket" Menge. Reflecting on these things, Leonard, draped in his gray blanket, watched anxiously from the substitutes' bench while Jake, the trainer, restored Kendall with a sopping sponge and, behind him, the Alton supporters cheered encouragingly. After all, Leonard told himself, this was only the beginning and Lorimer's superiority might be more apparent than real. It took more than age and weight and bright yellow head-guards to win a football game!

Lorimer had won the toss and given the ball to Alton. Garrick had kicked off and his effort had scarcely reached the enemy's twenty-yard line. From there it had been run back some five yards. Lorimer had tried the Alton center and made less than two. Then she had punted and the ball had gone out at Alton's forty. Joe Greenwood had made three at the right of the visitor's center, Kendall had lost a yard on a try at left end and Carpenter had punted to Lorimer's twenty-eight. Then the enemy had thrown an unexpected forward-pass from regular formation on first down and made it good for twenty-three yards, Captain Emerson pulling down the receiver just over the center line. Then the visitor's big full-back had torn through for that astounding gain, and now, with the game less than five minutes old, the enemy was almost inside the scoring zone.

Lorimer used a four-square backfield formation and a last-minute shift that was difficult for the opponent to follow. As the game went on she varied the direct pass by a snapback to the quarter, and a delayed pass following the latter proceeding accounted for several gains. Most of all, however, Lorimer had experienced players with weight and speed, which is a combination difficult to beat, and the game went badly for the Gray-and-Gold during that first half. Although a stand was made on the twenty-two-yard line that held the invaders for three downs and necessitated a try for a field-goal that failed, Alton's moment of humiliation was only postponed. It came finally soon after the beginning of the second period. An exchange of punts had gained a slight advantage for Lorimer and the "Yellow-Tops," as they were now being called in the stands, had twice made their distance, putting the ball down on Alton's forty-one yards. Then came a play that fooled the home team badly. What had every appearance of being a plunge by left half through his own side, with the whole Lorimer backfield in it, proved a moment later to be the old hidden ball stunt, with the long-legged Lorimer quarter sneaking around the other end and no one paying any heed to him. The whole Alton team had been pulled to the right, and the runner had a clear field for several precious moments. When Carpenter tackled him he was only seventeen yards from the last line.

That misadventure seemed to place the defenders of the north goal in a condition of consternation from which they didn't wholly recover until the enemy had pushed the ball across. It took them but seven plays to do it, concentrating on Smedley and Butler and using their battering full-back for four of the seven assaults. It was a sad sight to the Alton sympathizers on stands and bench, for the Gray-and-Gold warriors looked strangely helpless and their efforts to repel the attack only half-hearted. Yet, scarcely a minute later, those same warriors broke through the enemy line and spoiled the try-at-goal, a feat that had seemed impossible!

With the score at 6 to 0 the game went on to the whistle that ended the second period, Alton battling fiercely to reach the Lorimer goal and never getting nearer than the thirty-six yards. Lorimer appeared willing to cry quits for the balance of the half, kicking on second down and seeming satisfied to play on the defensive. It was a penalty against the visitor for holding that aided Alton in penetrating as far into the enemy territory as the thirty-six. There, with two to go on fourth down, Captain Emerson, faking a placement kick, threw over the line. Menge, however, who was to have taken the pass, failed to get into position and the ball grounded. The half ended there.

Leonard plodded back to the gymnasium with the others and sat around and felt very small and useless. There had been plenty of minor casualties, and Jake was busy all during the intermission. Coach Cade talked earnestly to this player and that and finally to them all. He didn't say much. He told them, in effect, that they were playing a mighty good team and there was no disgrace attached to the touchdown that had been scored against them. He said that in the next half they would find it easier to stop Lorimer's rushes, now that they knew her game better, and that he didn't see why they shouldn't be able to score a couple of times themselves. "Of course," he added quietly, "you'll have to play very differently from the way you've been playing, fellows. I'm willing to take my share of the blame, but there isn't one of you with enough assurance to tell me that you played that half the way I've taught you to play! You tried out a system of your own. And it didn't work. Now, then let's try the other style of football, the sort you've been learning for the last two years. Watch the ball and not the players. You've been fooled so often you ought to have enough by now! And when you have the ball start sooner. Don't let the other fellows stop you on your side of the line. And play hard, fellows, *hard*! Why, you haven't any of you perspired yet! Come on out now and show those big guys what a lot of poor shrimps they are!"

Of course what ought to have happened then is this. Alton, inspired by the coach's words, filled with a new courage and a greater determination, returned to the field and trampled the foe underfoot, showing a startling reversal of form and winning the game by an overwhelming score. Well, maybe, but it didn't happen that way so any one could notice it. This is a truthful narrative, and facts are facts.

The line-up for the third period was the same as for the first with the exception of Stimson at left guard in place of the much-battered

Smedley. There were plenty of other changes before the game came to an end, but they were not yet. Lorimer kicked off and Kendall caught and was downed after a twelve-yard run-back. Carpenter sent Greenwood at the line and Joe hit something hard and bounced back. Menge got three outside left tackle and Carpenter punted short to midfield. Lorimer made her distance and placed the pigskin on Alton's forty-two. A delayed pass lost a yard. A plunge at left tackle was smeared by Stimson. Lorimer kicked to the ten yards and Carpenter ran back to his seventeen. Kendall got through on the right of the line for six yards. Kendall tried the same place again and was stopped. Carpenter ran wide around his left and gained two. Kendall punted and the Lorimer quarter was thrown in his tracks by Emerson. Lorimer started back from her twenty-four yards and found a soft place at Wells, making it first down on her thirty-seven. Another try at Wells was good for only a yard. Lorimer then threw forward, but the pass was knocked down by Staples. A second forward to the other side of the field grounded. Lorimer punted.

And so the game went. Alton was playing better and harder, but she couldn't make much headway at that. Carpenter seemed unwilling to attempt variety in the plays he ordered, and Lorimer solved most of them before they started. Several penalties were meted out, both teams sharing about equally. The third period ended with the ball in Alton's possession on her own forty-yard line. With ten minutes left to play, a victory for the home team was scarcely within the possibilities, while, on the other hand, it was very generally predicted that Lorimer would not be able to add to her holdings.

Five fresh players went in for Alton. Newton succeeded Garrick at center, Renneker gave way to Raleigh, Wells to Wilde, Carpenter to Appel and Kendall to Reilly. Leonard, who had expected to see the hard-fighting Goodwin replace young Menge at left half before this, was surprised to observe "Cricket" still in place when the whistle blew again. Appel proved an improvement over Carpenter right away. "Bee," as Slim had once remarked, had a sting, and it wasn't long before Lorimer experienced it. The new quarter appeared to possess no awe of the enemy. He banged "Red" Reilly into the line once and then called for a risky double-pass play that threw Menge around the enemy right end with almost a clear field ahead of him. The Lorimer right half nipped the play and stood the diminutive Cricket on his head after a seven-yard gain, but Alton cheered loudly and triumphantly and took heart. But the Alton advance ended four plays later when Reilly fumbled and a Lorimer back shot through and fell on the rolling ball. Lorimer worked to Alton's thirty-one, was held for three downs and attempted a desperate placement kick that fell five yards short. Seven of the last ten minutes were gone when a short forward-pass straight over the middle of the line gave Emerson a chance to dodge his way for a dozen yards and put the pigskin down on the enemy's thirty-four.

Carpenter had twice tried the new plays for no results, and now Appel had a go at one of them. The one he selected was a half-back run from close formation, the ball going to quarter and from him to one of three players running past him and turning in around a boxed end. The chief merit of it lay in the fact that the ball was well hidden and the play could be made fast. Much, naturally, depended on the work of the linemen in doing away with the enemy defense. The ball went to the second runner in the tandem, who might be either one of the backs. The first man's duty was to clear away the enemy's secondary defense long enough for the man with the ball to get clear of the line. After that it was mainly up to the latter to look after himself, although, theoretically at least, he was protected from behind.

Appel chose this play—Number 39 was its official title—with the ball on Lorimer's thirty-four-yard line well over toward the west side of the field. Cricket Menge was second in line when the backs turned as the ball was snapped and ran past the quarter. The play was nearly spoiled by Slim's inability to throw the opposing end in, but he did the next best thing and allowed him to go past on the outside. Reilly took the Lorimer right half and disposed of him neatly and Cricket piled around on his heels. Greenwood prevented a flank attack and then confusion reigned and for a moment no one could have said exactly what did happen. But when the moment—a brief one—had passed, there was Cricket running two yards ahead of the nearest pursuer and making straight for the goal. It was Appel who put the crowning touch on his work by spurting through the ruck and engaging the Lorimer quarter just in time. Menge, small and fleet, reached the goal-line an instant later almost unchallenged. And after that the Gray-and-Gold held firmly against the charge of a frantic opponent and Rus Emerson dropped the ball very neatly between the uprights and well over the bar, doing what Lorimer had failed to do on a like occasion and so winning a game that, viewing the matter without prejudice, belonged to the enemy!

CHAPTER VIII
A STRANGE RESEMBLANCE

The school weekly, *The Doubleay*—more generally referred to as the "*Flubdub*"—was almost epic over the Lorimer game in the following Thursday's issue. It dwelt heavily on the dramatic aspects and very lightly on the scientific. It found, or pretended to find, much encouragement in the masterly way in which the Alton representatives had overcome the enemy's lead and soared to victory in the last minutes of play. Every one came in for a kind word—every one save the adversaries—and there was even fulsome praise for a few: Captain Emerson and Appel and Cricket Menge and Greenwood and Gordon Renneker. Even Slim, who had stuck it out for three periods, was mentioned approvingly. The *Flubdub* concluded with a flourish of trumpets, declaring that the Alton team had already found its stride and was headed straight for a victory over Kenly Hall.

The *Flubdub's* effusion is set forth here, out of chronological order, merely to show how judgments differ. There were others who viewed the Lorimer game with less enthusiasm; as, for instance, Slim and Leonard. Slim made a wry face and shrugged his shoulders. "Just plain robbery," said the left end. "We hadn't any more right to take that game than—than nothing at all! Talk about stealing the baby's rattle! Why, bless my soul, General, the only reason that '39' play succeeded was because it went wrong! I was supposed to box that end of theirs, Kellog, and he wouldn't box. By rights, he ought to have swung around back of me and spoiled the picture. Just by luck he didn't, and Cricket got by and squirmed loose. That wasn't good football, son, it was good luck. We played pretty fairly punk, the lot of us, although we did do a bit better after Appel took the helm. Bee isn't the player Carpenter is, but he certainly can run the team a sight better, if you want my opinion. As for me, I don't mind owning that I was rotten. But all the others were, too, so I don't feel so badly. Even your friend Renneker did more heavy looking on than anything else, so far as I could see."

"I'm afraid I can't claim him as a friend," said Leonard. "He's never known me since we parted in the cab that day."

"Well, I'm beginning to sour on that handsome guy as a tackle. Looks to me like he was touched with frost!"

At about the same time that Saturday evening Rus Emerson was seated in Coach Cade's front room in the old white house opposite the school gate on Academy street. Johnny sat at one side of a big mahogany table and Rus at the other, and each was slumped well down on his spine as if he had put in a hard day's work. The soft light of the lamp left their faces in shadow. The coach was speaking. "Who makes up these All-Scholastic Football Teams, Cap?" he inquired.

"The papers, I guess. That is, the sports editors."

"Reckon they make mistakes now and then?"

"I wouldn't wonder." Rus smiled gently in the shadow.

"H'm." There was silence a moment. Then: "He certainly looks good," continued the coach almost wistfully. "I don't know that I ever saw a chap who came nearer to looking the part of a clever, hard-fighting lineman. Why, just on appearances you'd pick him out of a crowd and shake hands with yourself."

"He certainly does look the part," agreed Rus. "And maybe he will find his pace after a bit."

"Maybe." But Johnny's tone was dubious. "He won't find it unless he looks for it, though, and it doesn't seem to me that he's taking the trouble to look." The coach laughed softly, ruefully. "The funny thing is, Cap, that he's got me bluffed. I know mighty well that he needs jacking up, but every time I get ready to ask him if he won't kindly come alive and take an interest in things he turns that calmly superior gaze on me and I haven't the courage. Why, drat his handsome hide, Cap, he looks like he *invented* football! Speaking harshly to him would be like—like knocking off the President's hat with a snowball!"

Rus chuckled. "He's got me like that, too. I want to apologize every time I open my mouth to him. Do you know, I'm beginning to wonder whether it wouldn't be a good plan to switch him over to the subs for a few days. It might be good medicine."

"Ye-es, it might. We'll see how he comes on the first of the week, though. Besides, Cap, who's going to tell him he's out of the line-up?" laughed Johnny. "Me, I'd have to write him a letter or send him a telegram!"

There was a knock at the door and Tod Tenney came in. "Hello, Coach! Hi, Rus! Say, is there anything special this evening? Anything to discuss, I mean? If there isn't I want to cut. There's a shindig down town." Tod grinned.

"'Nobody knows,'" hummed Rus, "'where the Old Man goes, but he takes his dancing shoes!'"

"Yes, there's one thing," answered the coach gravely. "I'd like your opinion, Tod. What do you think of this fellow Renneker?"

Tod already had the doorknob in hand, and now he turned it, pulled the portal inward and sort of oozed through the aperture. But before the countenance quite disappeared the mouth opened and the oracle spoke.

"He's a false-alarm," was the verdict.

Then the door closed.

Sunday afternoon Slim and Leonard went to walk again and, at Leonard's suggestion, ended up at Number 102 Melrose avenue. Johnny McGrath seemed extremely pleased to see them, but Slim had to hint broadly before the lemonade pitcher appeared. They talked of yesterday's game, which Johnny had attended. "I took my kid brother," said Johnny. "He plays on his grammar school team now and then. He's a sort of tenth substitute or something, as near as I get it. Well, he told me confidentially yesterday after we got home that his team could beat the stuffing out of ours!"

Slim laughed. "I wouldn't want to say it couldn't, the way we played yesterday. How does it happen, though, that the kid's playing football when you can't, Johnny?"

Johnny smiled. "Mother doesn't know it, you see. Maybe I ought to tell on him, but he's crazy about it and I haven't the heart. Sure, I don't believe he's likely to get hurt, for all the playing he does."

"Nor I. I just wondered. I do wish you could talk your mother around, though."

"Why," answered Johnny, "if I was to tell her I'd set my heart on it she'd not forbid me, Slim. But she'd be fearful all the time, and she's had worry enough. And it isn't like I cared much about it. Maybe I'd be a mighty poor football player, do you see? And, anyway, there's basket ball, and baseball, too."

"I didn't know you played baseball," said Slim.

"In the summer. We have a team here in town called the Crescents. I play second. Most of the fellows are older than me. It's a good team, too."

"Sure," said Slim. "I've heard of the Crescents. Some of the fellows from the carpet mills are on it, eh?"

"Most of them are mill fellows; McCarty and O'Keefe and McCluer and Carnochan—"

"How come you don't call yourselves the Shamrocks? Or the Sinn Feiners?"

"Well," laughed Johnny, "our pitcher's name is Cartier and the shortstop's is Kratowsky. And then there's—"

"Don't," begged Slim, "I can't bear it! Who do you play against?"

"Oh, any one. We played about thirty games last summer and won more than half. We go away for a lot of them. We went as far as Bridgeport once. We played twice at New Haven and once at New London and—" Johnny stopped and pushed a slice of lemon around the bottom of his glass with the straw. "Say, what's the name of the big fellow who's playing left—no, right guard for us?"

"Renneker," said Slim. "First name's Gordon. What about him?"

"Nothing. Gordon Renneker, eh? Does he play baseball, do you know?"

"No, I don't, Johnny. Want him for the Crescents next summer?"

Johnny shook his head. "I was—I was just wondering. You see, there was a fellow played on this New London team—the Maple Leaf it was called—looked a whole lot like this chap."

"Maybe it was he," said Slim cheerfully, setting down his glass with a regretful glance at the empty pitcher. "Maybe baseball's his real game and he got mixed."

"This fellow's name was Ralston, George Ralston," replied Johnny, frowning. "Sure, though, he was the dead spit of Renneker."

"I've heard of fellows changing their names before this," said Leonard. "Perhaps, for some reason, Renneker didn't want to play under his own name. Was he good, McGrath?"

"He was," answered their host emphatically. "He played first, and he had a reach from here to the corner of the porch and could hit the cover off the ball every time. He played fine, he did. Kind of a lazy-acting fellow; looked like he wasn't much interested. And maybe he wasn't, if what they told us was so."

"What was that?" asked Slim, smothering a yawn.

"Well, it was the newsboy on the train handed me the story. I wouldn't like to say he was giving me straight goods, for he was a mean looking little guy. You see, those Maple Leafs beat us, something like 14 to 6 it was, and some of our crowd were kind of sore. Going back on the train they were talking over the game and this newsboy was hanging around. Pretty soon he came over to where I was sitting and got to talking. Seemed he lived in New London, or else he hung over there. Anyway, he knew some of the players, and he got to telling about them. 'That fellow Smith,' he said—that wasn't the name, but he was talking about the pitcher—'gets thirty for every game.' 'Thirty what?' I asked, not getting him. 'Thirty dollars,' said he. 'No wonder we couldn't hit him then,' I said. 'And how about the catcher?' 'Oh, he don't get paid,' said the boy. 'They don't any of the others get paid except that Ralston guy. They give him twenty-five. He don't play regular with them, though.' I let him talk, not more than half believing him. Of course, I'd heard of fellows taking money for playing on teams supposed to be strictly amateur, but it's always on the quiet and you don't know if it's so. Afterwards I told Ted McCluer what I'd heard and Ted said he guessed it was straight goods; that he'd heard that that pitcher wasn't playing for his health."

Slim frowned and shook his head. "I guess you are mistaken, Johnny," he said. "Renneker's rather a swell, as I understand it, and it isn't likely he'd be running around the country playing ball for a trifling little old twenty-five dollars. Guess you're barking up the wrong tree, son."

"I'm not barking at all," replied Johnny, untroubled. "Only when I had a close look at this Renneker fellow yesterday he was so much like Ralston that I got to thinking."

"Well, I'd quit," advised Slim with some emphasis. "And I'd be mighty careful not to tell that yarn to any one else. You know how long Renneker would last if it got around."

Johnny nodded. "That's a fact," he agreed.

Leonard looked puzzled. "But if he isn't the fellow McGrath took him for, how could it matter any?"

"You aren't Julius Cæsar," answered Slim, "but you might have a hard time proving it."

"Get out! Cæsar's dead!"

"So are you—from the neck up," retorted Slim. "Come on home before you get any worse."

"I suppose, now," said Johnny thoughtfully, "they'd not let Renneker play on the team if it happened that he really was this other guy."

"Of course they wouldn't," answered Slim, a bit impatiently. "What do you think? Accepting money for playing baseball! I'll say they wouldn't! But I tell you you're all wrong about it, anyway, Johnny. So don't talk about it, son. Even if a fellow is innocent, getting talked about doesn't help him any."

"Sure, I know," agreed Johnny. "It wouldn't be him, I guess."

"Not a chance," said Slim heartily. "Coming, General?"

Half a block down the avenue Leonard broke the silence. "Sort of funny," he remarked, "that the initials should be the same. 'G. R.'; Gordon Renneker and George Ralston."

"Too blamed funny," muttered Slim.

Leonard looked at him with surprise. "You don't think, do you, that—that there's anything in it?"

Slim hesitated a moment. Then: "Don't know what to think," he answered. "Johnny's no fool. If you play baseball with a chap you get a pretty good view of him. Of course, now and then you find a case where two fellows look so much alike their own mothers mightn't know them apart at first, and Johnny might easily be mistaken. I dare say he didn't get a very good look at Renneker yesterday. Besides, what would a chap like Renneker be doing barnstorming around for a measly twenty-five?" It was evident to Leonard that Slim was working hard to convince himself. "Anyway," he went on, "Johnny'll keep it to himself after this."

"Yes," Leonard affirmed, "but I think he still believes he's right."

"Let him, so long as he keeps it to himself. I'm not awfully enthusiastic about this Gordon Renneker, General. So far he hasn't shown anything like what you'd expect from a fellow with his reputation. And I don't warm up to him much in other ways. He seems a pretty cold fish. But he may get better, and, even if he doesn't, I guess we wouldn't want to lose him. So it's up to us to forget all about this silly pipe-dream of Johnny's, see?"

"I see," replied the other thoughtfully.

Something in his tone caused Slim to dart a questioning glance at him, but Leonard's countenance added nothing to his voice and they went on in silence.

CHAPTER IX
LEONARD MAKES A TACKLE

Monday was a day of rest for those who had taken part for any length of time in the Lorimer game, and so the two teams that finally faced each other for a short scrimmage contained much doubtful talent. Leonard again went in at left tackle and, since he didn't have Billy Wells and Captain Emerson to oppose him, he managed to do a great deal better. Cruikshank, who acted as quarterback and captain of the patched-up eleven on which Leonard found himself, twice thumped the latter on his back and uttered hoarse words of approval. The two teams were very nearly matched, and the ten minute period was nearly over before either secured a chance to score. Then A Team got Dakin off tackle for a gallop of sixteen yards, and the pigskin lay close to the opponent's twenty. Goodwin slashed through center for four and Dakin got two. Then Goodwin tried the middle of the line again and found no hole, and there was a yard loss. Goodwin, who had been playing full-back until recently, had not yet fully mastered his new job. With five to go on third down, Cruikshank took the ball himself and managed to squeeze through the enemy's right wing and squirm along for the rest of the distance. The ball was then close to the ten-yard line. Kerrison dropped back from end position to the eighteen and held out his arms. But no one was fooled by that gesture, and Dakin, plunging past Leonard, made less than a yard. Then it was "Kerrison back!" once more, and this time Leonard got the jump on the opposing guard and Dakin found a hole to his liking and plunged through to the four yards. With less than three to go, Kerrison went back to end position and on the next play the whole backfield concentrated behind Goodwin, and once more Leonard put his man out and felt the runner rasping by him. The opposition melted, and Goodwin went through and staggered well past the goal-line before he was downed. The coach wouldn't let them try the goal, and so they had to be satisfied with the six points. They trotted back to the gymnasium fairly contented, however.

Leonard secretly hoped that his performance, even though against a none too strong adversary, had been noted by Johnny. If it had the fact was known only to the coach and no immediate results materialized. On Tuesday, with the first-string men back in place, Leonard wasn't called on; although he had plenty of work with C Squad. There was a second cut that afternoon and the number of candidates left was barely sufficient for three elevens. Of that number, however, was Leonard, even though, as he assured himself, better players had been banished!

Wednesday found him again at tackle, but now on the right of the line, with Stimson at one elbow and Gurley dodging back and forth at his other side. He found Butler less trying as a vis à vis than Billy Wells, but he somehow wished Johnny hadn't changed him over. Billy, even at his deadliest, was an honorable foe, and even a partial success gained against Billy was something to be proud of. Not, however, that Leonard found Butler an easy adversary. Far from it. Butler made Leonard look pretty poor more than half the time, while, when Leonard was obliged to give his attention to Left Guard Smedley, the substitute tackle made an even sorrier showing. On the whole, Leonard wasn't a bit proud of his work, either on offense or defense, during the first period, and returned to the bench convinced that his goose was cooked. When Johnny, criticizing and correcting along the line of panting players, reached Leonard he stopped again.

"Not so good to-day," he said. "What was wrong, Grant?"

Leonard hadn't the least idea what was wrong, beyond a general inability to play the position as it should be played, and, besides, he was horribly surprised and embarrassed by the unexpected attention. Nevertheless, after a moment of open-mouthed dumbness, he had a flash of inspiration.

"I don't think I can play so well at left tackle, sir," he replied, meeting the coach's eyes with magnificent assurance. Mr. Cade smiled very slightly and moved past. But he turned his face again toward Leonard an instant later.

"I'll take you up on that, Grant," he said sharply.

Leonard felt uncomfortable. He wasn't quite certain what Johnny had meant. Besides, there had been something—well, not exactly unfriendly, but sort of—sort of rasping in his tone; as if Johnny had thought to himself, "Get sassy with me, will you. I'll show you!"

Leonard wished now he had kept his mouth shut. Some of the fellows who had taken part in the first period of scrimmaging were making their way back to the showers, but as no one dismissed him Leonard sat still and got his breath back and wondered what awaited him. Then Tod Tenney called "Time up, Coach!" and Johnny Cade swung around and pulled out his little book and sent them back on the field again.

"B Team," he called. "Gurley and Kerrison, ends; Wilde and Grant, tackles; Squibbs and—"

But Leonard didn't hear any more. He was shedding his blanket and telling himself fiercely that he just had to make good now. The fierceness remained throughout the subsequent twenty-one minutes required to play ten minutes of football. At the first line-up Billy Wells smiled joyfully at Leonard. "See who's here," he called gayly, swinging his big arms formidably. "Who let you in, sonny? Some one sure left the gate open! Which way are you coming?"

"Inside," answered Leonard grimly.

"Welcome to our midst, sweet youth!"

Of course Leonard didn't go inside. In the first place, the play was around the right end, and in the next place Billy wouldn't have stood for it. Leonard busied himself with Renneker, got slammed back where he belonged and then plunged through the melting lines and chased after the play. Rus Emerson slapped him on the back as they passed on their way to the next line-up.

"Glad to see you, Grant," declared the captain.

On the next play Leonard and Billy mixed it up thoroughly, but truth compels the admission that of the two Leonard was the most mixed! You just couldn't get under Billy. If you played low, Billy played lower. If you feinted to your right, Billy moved to his right, too. If you tried to double-cross him and charged the way you feinted he outguessed you and was waiting. He knew more ways of using his shoulder than there were letters in the alphabet, and his locked hands coming up under your chin were most effective. No cat was half as quick as Billy and no bull-dog half as stubborn and tenacious. Yet Leonard did have his infrequent triumphs. Once, when Reilly wanted three yards to make the distance, Leonard put Billy Wells out completely and Red slid by for a yard more than needed. Leonard had got the jump that time by a fraction of a second, and he was so proud of his feat that doubtless it showed on his face, for Billy viewed him sarcastically for a moment and then announced: "Just bull-luck, you poor half portion of prunes!"

Leonard paid for that moment of success two plays later when his chin got in the way of Billy's elbow. They had to call time for Leonard, for an accidental blow on the point of the chin eliminates ambition for all of a minute. But he got up with ambition returning fast and gave Billy a promising look that brought a grin to that youth's countenance. "Atta boy," he approved. "Lots more waiting!"

If there was Leonard didn't go after it. Instead, he was more careful to keep his head down. A leather helmet can take a lot of punishment without showing it. A few minutes later, after A Squad had taken the ball away and pushed herself down to B's twenty-six yards, Leonard had the supreme satisfaction of smearing a play aimed at him. Billy came through all right, for Leonard let him, but the hole closed behind him, and if Leonard felt any compunction because his cleats were digging into the lower extremities of the fallen Billy he didn't show it! That time Billy viewed his adversary ponderingly as he accepted the proffered hand and scrambled to his feet.

"Huh," he said, "the kid's getting on, eh?"

Leonard grinned. "On to you, Wells," he answered.

But these great moments were few and far between. Generally Billy was too good for the neophyte. Usually if there was a gain needed where Leonard held forth, that gain eventuated, although it wasn't always as big as expected. Stimson helped his tackle in many a hard place, and Goodwin, playing behind, could be depended on to quell a too ambitious runner. Oddly enough, when Leonard found Renneker in front of him, as happened when A Squad spread her line open, he wasn't nearly so concerned. Renneker, in spite of size and weight and reputation, could be fooled and, after a fashion, handled. Renneker was slow, for one thing. There was no doubt about that. The A Squad quarter was forever telling him so, even if

Leonard hadn't discovered the fact for himself. Leonard could handle Renneker far better when A had the ball than he could Billy Wells.

A Squad fought desperately to a touchdown and then added a goal. As she had already scored once in the first period, she was entitled to be a trifle lordly, which she was. B Squad kicked off again and Cricket Menge, catching near his five-yard line, raced back up the field, miraculously worming his fleet way through most of the enemy forces. At the forty yards he was still going, with his own players building a hasty interference about him and the B Squad players converging on him from all points, mostly from behind. Forced close to the side-lines near the center of the field, Cricket swung out from behind his interference and started across. Gurley dived for him and missed him. Cricket straightened out for the distant goal, still running hard and fast. Leonard and Reilly drew up on him as he passed the forty-yard line, and Appel, the B Squad quarter, hovered anxiously ahead. It was a confused rabble of friend and foe that scuttled down the field. Leonard tried hard to get around Greenwood, plunging along in Menge's wake, but the big full-back held him away over two white lines. Reilly, edging in, dove too soon and went over and over. Greenwood, striving to hurdle the obstacle, faltered long enough for Leonard to thrust past him. Kendall threw himself in Leonard's way, but the latter hurdled over him. He was a bare three yards behind the runner now, and the thirty-yard mark was underfoot. Appel was edging over, yet not making the mistake of leaving his goal too far. Leonard was too tuckered to do much planning. He put every ounce of strength into a last supreme effort, gained a little and plunged forward, arms out-thrust and fingers groping.

His left hand closed on something tightly, he felt himself being dragged along the turf. Then Appel landed on Cricket's back, and the race was over. Cricket turned a reproachful countenance toward Leonard when they had pulled him to his unsteady feet. But he managed a grin. So did Leonard. That was about all he could have managed just then, for his head was going around, his lungs were bursting and his stomach was horribly empty. He was infinitely relieved when he discovered that the battle was over and that, having been assisted to his feet, he could make his uncertain way to the bench. He passed Coach Cade on the way, and the coach met his eyes and nodded. At least, Leonard thought he did. He was too exhausted to be certain of it.

CHAPTER X
THE SECOND TEAM COMES OVER

That incident seemed to bring about a subtle difference in Leonard's relations with the other players. He received no particular praise for what, indeed, was only a part of the day's work; probably none besides Appel and Slim referred to it; but the next day he noticed that many more of the fellows spoke to him or nodded to him in the gymnasium, on the way to the field or during practice. Jim Newton even hailed him as "General," having probably heard Slim use that nickname. But Wednesday's performance appeared to have made no difference in Leonard's standing on the squad. To-day he relieved Lawrence for the last five minutes of the last scrimmage period, and that was all the attention he received from Johnny. Billy Wells nodded to him, but had nothing to say. That was Leonard's last appearance in the line-up that week, for on Friday only the first- and second-string players got into the brief practice. On Saturday the eleven went to Hillsport and played Hillsport School, winning an easy contest by a score of 14 to 0. Leonard didn't go along, although some half-hundred of the fellows did. Instead, he and a half-dozen others whose presence at Hillsport had not been considered necessary by the coach spent an hour or more on the field with a ball and they went across to the second team gridiron and saw the last half of a ragged game between the scrubs and a team of substitutes from the Alton High School. Slim showed up just before supper time with two broad strips of plaster over his right cheekbone.

It was on Sunday that Leonard first heard reference to the Sophomore Dinner. "By the way," said Slim, looking up from the book he was reading—it was raining, and the usual Sunday afternoon walk was out of the question—"have you come across for the dinner yet, General?"

"Eh?" asked Leonard. "What dinner?"

"The class dinner. You're going, of course."

"Do you mean our class? I hadn't heard about it!"

"Oh, that's so; the notices aren't out yet, are they? Well, it's to be the seventh of next month. I forgot this was your first year with us, old son. It's always the first Saturday in November."

"First I've heard of it. How much does it cost?"

"A dollar and a half this year. It used to be a dollar, but they put up the price on us. You'll get your money's worth, though."

"Why, I suppose I'll go. Does every one? All the fellows in the class, I mean."

"Pretty much. A few pikers stay away. Same with all the class feeds, I guess."

"Do you mean that all the classes have these dinners?"

"Sure. We have ours in November, the freshies have theirs in February, the juniors in April and the seniors in June, just before Class Day."

"Where do we have it?" asked Leonard.

"Kingman's this year. There are only about two places, Kingman's restaurant and the Alton House. Last year we had the freshman feed at the Alton House, and it wasn't very good."

"Is it fun?"

"Sure it is. Especially when the freshies try to break it up! Last year the sophs had their shindig at Kingman's and we smuggled Billy Wells into the basement in the afternoon and he hid behind a pile of boxes until about seven o'clock and then unscrewed the electric light switch. We came rather near getting into trouble over that. The sophs were upstairs, on the second floor, and of course we didn't want to put the lights out all over the building, but we had to do it. Mr. Kingman was tearing mad and made a holler to faculty. It ended with an apology from the freshman class, though, for Kingman thought it over, I suppose, and realized that if he made too much of a fuss we'd stop going to his place. Billy almost got caught getting out that night. He was sneaking out the back way when he ran into one of the cooks. Billy swears the man had a cleaver in his hand. Anyway, Billy got behind a door or into a corner and they didn't see

71

him." Slim chuckled. "The sophs didn't get on with their banquet for nearly an hour."

"But what's the idea?" asked Leonard. "Why did you want to bust up their party?"

Slim pondered a moment. Then he shook his head. "I don't know. It's just a custom. It's always been done, I guess."

"And do the sophs do the same thing when the freshmen have their blow-out?"

"Oh, no, that would be beneath our dignity. But we try to make things a little difficult for the juniors."

"I see." Leonard smiled. "Then, after I've paid my dollar and a half, I can't be quite certain that I'll get my dinner, eh?"

"Oh, you'll get it," answered Slim confidently. "No silly bunch of freshies is going to bust up this party, son! We'll see to that. And that reminds me. Keep your ears open from now on and if you hear anything let me know."

"Hear anything?"

"Yes. You might, you know. Freshies like to talk big, and one of them might let drop some information that would be of interest to us. Of course, they'll try something, you know, and it would make it easier for us if we got an inkling beforehand so we'd know what to look for."

"I see," said Leonard. "I suppose you, as Class President, are sort of responsible for the success of the affair, Slim."

"Well, I'm chairman of the dinner committee, and about half of our duty is to see that the freshies don't hurl a monkey-wrench into the machinery, so to speak. Know any freshmen?"

"Two or three, but only to speak to."

"Well, it would be a good plan to get better acquainted," said Slim. "It's an older fellow's duty to be friendly with the freshies and make life pleasant for them, you know."

Leonard grinned. "And keep his ears open? Sort of like playing the spy, isn't it?"

"Of course. There'll be a lot of spying done on both sides during the next fortnight. They'll be trying to find out where we're going to feed, and when, and we'll be trying to find out what they're going to do about it."

"But if we get out notices, as you said we did, what's to keep the freshmen from knowing all about it?"

"The notices don't give the date and place, General. They're just reminders to the members of the class. Of course, the freshmen do find out easy enough, but it makes them work harder if we don't tell 'em. There's one thing they won't do, anyway, and that's cut off the light. Mr. Kingman will take mighty good care that no one gets into the cellar this year!"

"What will they do, do you suppose?" asked Leonard.

"Search me! Maybe they'll try to rush the hall. They did that three or four years ago, they say, and ate most of the dinner before the sophs could get them out again!"

"Gee," murmured Leonard, "I can't imagine this year's bunch of freshies trying anything like that!"

"Well, you can't tell. They get pretty cocky after they've been here a month or so. Besides, they had their election last week, and that always sort of starts them going. There's a lot of them this year; nearly a hundred and thirty, I hear; and if they want to make trouble they can do it."

"How many of us are there, Slim?"

"Ninety—something; ninety-six, I think. Oh, we can look after ourselves. The most they can do, in any case, is hold things up for awhile."

"Sounds exciting," mused Leonard. "Do they ever get to scrapping?"

"Oh, no, not what you'd really call scrapping. Sometimes there's a rush and a few fellows get mussed up a little. There's no hard-feeling, you understand. It's just the freshmen's bounden duty to break up the sophomore party if they can do it. They never do, but they keep right on trying. It's rather fun, you know."

73

"Yes, but I guess I'll have a good feed before I go," laughed Leonard. "Then I'll be sure of not starving!"

He paid his dollar and a half to the class treasurer the next day and received the strictly confidential information that the dinner would take place on the evening of November 7th at Kingman's Restaurant at seven o'clock. "You understand, I guess," added Wilfred Cash, "that you're not to mention the place or the date to any one."

"Oh, quite," Leonard assured him gravely.

That Monday afternoon the second team, which for unavoidable reasons, one of which was the inability to find a coach, was nearly a fortnight late in getting under way, came over and faced the first. Many familiar faces were to be seen amongst the scrub aggregation, for fully half of the second team's line-up had tried for the big team and been rejected. Leonard, looking on at the scrimmage from the bench, still marveled that he was not taking orders from Mr. Fadden instead of from Mr. Cade.

The second's coach was an old Alton graduate and a resident of the town who, at the earnest solicitation of the Athletic Committee, had consented to give up several hours a day to the task of providing something for the school team to whet their claws on. He was in the real estate business and was a busy man, and that he had listened to the call of the committee was greatly to his credit; the more so that, although he had played football well at Alton and, afterwards, at Yale, he had grown out of touch with the game and was forced to make a study of its modern developments before he dared face his charges. That year's second team never quite reached the average of Alton second teams, but it was for no lack of hard work on the part of Mr. Fadden. He was quite a stout man, and the scrub was soon calling him "Tub," though never to his face; but when the second team was dissolved a month later the nickname was no longer deserved, since, however the players had fared, Mr. Fadden had lost some thirty pounds from a portion of his anatomy where it had been extremely noticeable.

Leonard had a few minutes of play at tackle and found himself opposed to a very tall and rather awkward youth named Lansing. Lansing wasn't difficult and Leonard had little trouble with him. In fact, the whole second team showed up pretty poorly that afternoon and the first scored three times in twenty minutes of scrimmage. The first might have done even better had she used her best line-up. As it was, most of those who had played against Hillsport on Saturday were not used.

With the advent of the scrub team Leonard's chance of getting into action was much diminished, as he speedily realized. There were, naturally, but two tackle positions on the first, and for those positions there were exactly six applicants, including Leonard Grant. Billy Wells was mortally certain of the right tackle position, and Butler or Wilde would get the other. That left Lawrence, Cash and Leonard himself. Probably Lawrence would be chosen for second substitute. It looked to Leonard as if he and Cash would be out of jobs in a very short time!

Theoretically, of course, those tackle positions were still open, but Leonard knew very well that, although he might conceivably give Lawrence and Cash—possibly even Wilde—a run for his money, he had no more chance of equalling Billy Wells or Sam Butler as a tackle than he had of displacing Johnny Cade as coach! It didn't seem to him that Slim's advice to become an applicant for a tackle position had been very good. Tackles were a drug on the market. Still, to be fair to Slim, so were guards! Well, he would just do the best he could and be satisfied with what he got. Perhaps he might manage to hang on by the skin of his teeth; and it would help him considerably next fall, he concluded, to finish this season out on the first team, even if he never got off the bench again.

With the Hillsport game out of the way, the season was half over and Alton metaphorically took a deep breath, cinched its belt up another hole and set its gaze on the Mt. Millard contest. Last year the neighboring institution, situated at Warren, some eighteen miles distant, had beaten Alton by the score of 10 to 0. Of course that was at the height—or perhaps bottom would be better—of Alton's historic slump, but the defeat had rankled. It rankled yet. Until two years ago Mt. Millard had been an adversary of no consequence. Then she had taken unto herself a new coach and won two games running, the first 19 to 0, the second 10 to 0. The fact that Alton hadn't been able to score against Mt. Millard in two years made it even worse. There was a very general sentiment at Alton this fall in favor of defeating Mt. Millard, and defeating her conclusively. In fact, Alton wanted Revenge, Revenge with a capital R! To that end, therefore, on Tuesday Johnny Cade set to work to strengthen his defense against the kicking and passing game, which was Mt. Millard's long suit. The offense was not neglected, but it was given second place in the week's program. By Thursday two changes, each of which looked to be permanent, had been made. Reilly had succeeded Kendall at right half and Appel had taken Carpenter's position at quarter. Several changes in the line were also tried, but none appeared more than tentative. Jim Newton was running Garrick very close for center and, strange to tell, Coach Cade on two occasions relegated Gordon Renneker to the subs and placed Raleigh at right guard. To an unbiased observer there seemed little choice between them, although they were notably different in build and style of playing. When practice ended Thursday afternoon, which it didn't do until it had become almost too dark to see the ball, it would have required a prophet of more than usual ability to predict the line-up that would face Mt. Millard.

That evening Slim took Leonard over to Lykes to see Rus Emerson. Leonard went none too eagerly, in spite of Emerson's invitation of some time ago, but he went. Afterwards he was very glad he had.

CHAPTER XI
ALTON SEEKS REVENGE

Number 16 was already pretty well crowded when Slim and the diffident Leonard entered. Captain Emerson was there, and so was his roommate, George Patterson. Then there was Billy Wells, Tod Tenney, Jim Newton, Gordon Renneker and a chap named Edwards who later turned out to be the baseball captain. As it seemed to be taken for granted that every one knew every one else Leonard was not introduced. He and Slim squeezed onto a bed beside Jim Newton—the thing squeaked threateningly but held—and Rus passed them a bottle of ginger-ale, with two straws, and a carton of biscuits. Having helped themselves to the biscuits, they passed it on to Newton. Jim, at the moment engaged in conversation with Tod Tenney, absent-mindedly set the box on the bed. After that it couldn't be found until Jim got up to go. And then it wasn't worth finding, for it had slipped down under the big chap and was no longer recognizable.

A good deal of "shop" was talked, in spite of Captain Emerson's repeated protests. The Mt. Millard game was discussed exhaustively. The only feature concerned with it that was not mentioned was the Alton line-up. That seemed to be taboo. Tod Tenney declared that if Alton didn't wipe the ground up with those fellows this time he'd resign and let the team go to the bow-wows. Whereupon Jim Newton gave a grunt and remarked that maybe if Tod resigned beforehand it would change their luck.

"Luck!" countered Tod. "It isn't your luck that's wrong, you big piece of cheese. You're scared of those fellows over at Warren. They've put the kibosh on you. Why, last year you didn't know whether you were on your head or your heels. They didn't have half the team that you had, and you went and let them lick the daylight out of you."

"Sic 'em, Prince!" murmured Stick Patterson.

"Oh, well," said Billy Wells confidently, "never mind last year, Tod. Keep your glimmers on Saturday's fracas. We're going to smear those lucky guys all over the field. We've got it on them in weight this year and—"

"We had last year, too, hadn't we?" asked Edwards.

"Not above the collar," grunted Tenney.

"For the love of Mike, fellows," begged Rus, "shut up on football. It's enough to play it every day without having to talk it all evening."

"What else do you expect football men to talk about?" asked Slim, rolling the empty ginger-ale bottle under Stick's bed. "You ought to know, Rus, that the football player's intellect isn't capable of dealing with any other subject."

"Dry up, Slim," said Billy Wells, "and move over, you poor insect. I want to talk to General Grant."

There being no room to move over without sitting in Jim Newton's lap, Slim crossed the room and took the arm of the Morris chair, just vacated by Billy. Billy squeezed onto the bed, securing another inch or two by digging Jim violently with an elbow. Jim grunted and said: "Little beast!" Billy turned a shrewd, smiling countenance on Leonard.

"Well, how's it going?" he asked.

"All right, thanks," answered Leonard vaguely. Just what "it" was he didn't know. Probably, however, life in general. But Billy's next words corrected the assumption.

"How long have you been playing the tackle position?" he asked.

"About three weeks," replied Leonard. "That explains it, doesn't it?" He added an apologetic smile.

"Explains what? Oh, I'm not ragging you, Grant. Why, say, you and I had some swell times! If you've been at it only three weeks, I'll say you're pretty good. But where'd you been playing?"

"Guard. I played guard two years at high school."

"Guard, eh?" Billy looked slightly puzzled. "Must have had a fairly light team, I guess. You don't look heavy enough for that, Grant."

"I am sort of light," sighed Leonard.

"Yes." Billy sized him up frankly. "You're quick, though, and I certainly like that. Had me guessing lots of times, I don't mind telling you."

"Oh, I don't know," Leonard murmured. "I'm pretty green at it."

"You'll do," said Billy. "But, say, mind if I give you a couple of tips? It may sound cheeky, but—"

"Gee, not a bit!" protested the other. "I wish you would. I—it's mighty good of you."

"Well, I don't pretend to know everything about playing tackle," Billy answered, "but there are one or two things I have learned, and I'm glad to pass them on to you, Grant, because you play a pretty nice game. Maybe if you were pressing me a bit closer for the position I wouldn't be so gabby." Billy grinned. "One thing is this, son. Watch the other fellow's eyes and not his hands. I noticed you kept looking at my hands or my arms. Don't do it. Not, at least, if you want to get the jump on your opponent. Watch his eyes, son. Another thing is, don't give yourself away by shifting too soon. You come forward every time with the foot that's going to take your weight. There are several ways of standing, and it's best to stand the way that suits you, but I like to keep my feet about even. That doesn't give me away. Then when I do start it's too late for the other fellow to do any guessing. See what I mean?"

Leonard nodded, but a little doubtfully. "I think so. But we were taught to put one foot well behind us so we'd have a brace if the opponent—"

"Sure, that's all right if you've got to let the other fellow get away first. But you don't need to. You start before he does, Grant. Look." Billy held his hands out, palms upward, elbows close to his body. "Come up under him like that, both legs under you until you're moving forward. Then step out, right or left, and get your leverage. Push him straight back or pivot him. You haven't given yourself away by moving your feet about or shifting your weight beforehand. You try it some time."

"I will, thanks," answered Leonard gratefully.

"And there's one more thing." There was a wicked glint in Billy's eyes. "Keep your head down so the other fellow can't get under your chin. I've known fellows to get hurt that way."

Leonard smiled. "So have I," he said.

Billy laughed and slapped him on the knee. "You'll do, General Grant," he declared. He turned to Jim Newton, and Leonard, considering what he had been told, didn't note for a moment that Gordon Renneker was speaking across the room to Slim. When he did, Renneker was saying:

"Baseball? No, very little. I've got a brother who goes in for it, though."

"Oh," replied Slim, "I thought maybe you pitched. You've sort of got the build, you know, Renneker. Hasn't he, Charlie?"

Charlie Edwards agreed that he had, looking the big guard up and down speculatively. Renneker shrugged his broad shoulders and smiled leniently. "Never tried it," he said in his careful way. "The few times I have played I've been at first. But I'm no baseball artist."

"First, eh?" commented Slim. "By Jove, you know, you ought to make a corking first baseman! Say, Charlie, you'd better get after him in the spring."

Edwards nodded and answered: "I certainly mean to, Slim."

Nevertheless it seemed to Leonard that the baseball captain's tone lacked enthusiasm. Slim, Leonard noted, was smiling complacently, and Leonard thought he knew what was in his chum's mind. Shortly after that the crowd broke up and on the way over to Haylow Slim asked: "Did you hear what Renneker said when I asked him if he played baseball?"

"Yes," said Leonard. Slim hadn't once mentioned the subject of Johnny McGrath's suspicions since that Sunday afternoon, and Leonard had concluded that the matter was forgotten. Now, however, it seemed that it had remained on Slim's mind, just as it had on his.

"He said," mused Slim, "that he didn't play. At least very little. Then he said that when he did play he played at first base. What do you make of that, General?"

"Very little. Naturally, if he should play baseball he'd go on first, with that height and reach of his. I noticed that Edwards didn't seem very keen about him for the nine."

"Yes, I noticed that, too." Slim relapsed into a puzzled silence. Then, at last, just as they reached the dormitory entrance, he added: "Oh, well, I guess Johnny just sort of imagined it."

"I suppose so," Leonard agreed. "Only, if he didn't—"

"If he didn't, what?" demanded Slim.

"Why, wouldn't it be up to us—or Johnny McGrath—to tell Mr. Cade or some one?"

"And get Renneker fired?" inquired Slim incredulously, as he closed the door of Number 12 behind him.

"Well, but, if he took money for playing baseball, Slim, he hasn't any right on the football team, has he? Didn't you say yourself that faculty would fire him if it was so, and they knew it?"

"If they knew it, yes," agreed Slim. "Now, look here, General, there's no sense hunting trouble. We don't know anything against Renneker, and so there's no reason for starting a rumpus. A fellow is innocent until he's proven guilty, and it's not up to us to pussyfoot about and try to get the goods on Renneker. Besides, ding bust it, there's only Johnny McGrath's say-so, and every one knows how—er—imaginative the Irish are!"

"All right," agreed Leonard, smiling. "Just the same, Slim, you aren't fooling me much. You believe there's something in Johnny's story, just as I do."

"Piffle," answered Slim. "Johnny's a Sinn Feiner. The Irish are all alike. They believe in fairies. You just can't trust the unsupported statement of a chap who believes in fairies!"

"You surely can work hard to fool yourself," laughed Leonard. "I suppose you're right, Slim, but it would be sort of rotten if one of the other schools got hold of it and showed Renneker up."

"Not likely, General. You stop troubling your brain about it. Best thing to do is forget it. That's what I'm going to do. Besides, I keep telling you there's nothing in it."

"I know. And I want to believe it just as much as you do, only—"

"There isn't any 'only!' Dry up, and put the light out!"

On Saturday Leonard was very glad indeed that, in Slim's words, there wasn't any 'only,' for without Gordon Renneker the Mt. Millard game might have ended differently. Renneker found himself in that contest. Slim always maintained that the explanation lay in the fact that Renneker's opponent, one Whiting, was, like Renneker, a big, slow-moving fellow who relied more on strength than speed; and Slim supported this theory by pointing out that in the last quarter, when a quicker and scrappier, though lighter, man had taken Whiting's place Renneker had relapsed into his customary form. Leonard reminded Slim that by that time Renneker had played a long, hard game and was probably tired out. Slim, however, remained unconvinced. But whatever the reason may have been, the big right guard on the Alton team played nice, steady football that Saturday afternoon. His work on defense was better than his performance when the Gray-and-Gold had the ball, just as it had been all season. He seemed to lack aggression in attack. But Coach Cade found encouragement and assured himself that Renneker could be taught to play a better offensive game by the time the Kenly Hall contest faced them. The big guard had been causing him not a little worry of late.

Mt. Millard brought over a clever, fast team that day. Her line was only a few pounds lighter than Alton's, but in the backfield the Gray-and-Gold had it all over her in weight, even when Menge was playing. Mt. Millard's backs were small and light, even her full-back running to length more than weight. Her quarter was a veritable midget, and if Alton had not witnessed his work for two years she might have feared for his safety amongst all those rough players! But Marsh was able to look after himself, as well as the rest of the team, and do it in a highly scientific manner. In spite of his diminutive size he was eighteen years of age and had played two seasons with Mt. Millard already. For that matter, the visitors presented a veteran team, new faces being few and far between.

Alton looked for trouble from the enemy's passing game and didn't look in vain. On the third play Mt. Millard worked a double pass that was good for nearly thirty yards and, less than eighty seconds after the whistle, was well into Alton territory. That fright—for it was a fright—put the home team on her mettle, and a subsequent play of a similar style was foiled with a loss of two yards. Mt. Millard was forced to punt from Alton's thirty-seven. Cricket Menge caught and made a startling run-back over three white lines. Then Alton tried her own attack and had slight difficulty in penetrating Mt. Millard's lighter line. Greenwood ripped his way through for three and four yards at a time and Reilly twice made it first down on plays off the tackles. It was Red's fumble near his own forty that halted that advance. Mt. Millard got the ball and started back with it.

From tackle to tackle the Alton line was invulnerable, save for two slight gains at Smedley's position. Mt. Millard's only chance, it seemed, was to run the ends, and that she did in good style until the opponent solved her plays and was able to stop them twice out of three times. But the visitor had brought along a whole bagful of tricks, and as the first period—they were playing twelve-minute quarters to-day—neared its end she opened the bag. Alton had plunged her way to the enemy's thirty-seven, and there Menge, trying to cut outside of left tackle, had become involved with his interference and been thrown for a two-yard loss. It was third down and six to go, and Joe Greenwood dropped back eight yards behind center and spread his hands invitingly. But the ball went to Reilly and Red cut the six yards down to three by a plunge straight at center. Goodwin went back once more, and this time took the pigskin. But, although he swung a long leg, the ball wasn't kicked. Instead it went sailing through the air to the side of the field where Menge was awaiting it. Unfortunately, though, Cricket was not the only one with a desire for the ball, and a fraction of a second before it was due to fall into his hands a long-legged adversary leaped upward and captured it. Cricket tackled instantly and with all the enthusiasm of an outraged soul and the long-legged one came heavily to earth, but the ball was back in the enemy's hands and again Alton's triumph had been checked.

One hopeless smash at the Gray-and-Gold line that netted less than a yard, and Mt. Millard opened her bag of tricks. Speaking broadly, there aren't any new plays in football and can't be except when an alteration of the rules opens new possibilities. What are called new plays are usually old plays revived or familiar plays in novel disguise. Mt. Millard, then, showed nothing strictly original that afternoon, but some of the things she sprang during the remainder of that game might almost as well have been fresh from the mint so far as effectiveness was concerned. During the minute or two that remained of the first period she made her way from her own thirty-two yards to Alton's sixteen in four plays, while the home team supporters looked on aghast. First there was a silly-looking wide-open formation with every one where he shouldn't have been, to meet which Alton rather distractedly wandered here and there and edged so far back that when, instead of the involved double or perhaps triple-pass expected, a small half-back took the ball from center and ran straight ahead with it, he found almost no opposition until he had crossed the scrimmage line. After that, that he was able to dodge and twirl and throw off tacklers until Billy Wells brought him down from behind just over the fifty-yard line, was owing to his own speed and cunning.

When Mt. Millard again spread wide Alton thought she knew what was coming, and this time her ends dropped back only some five yards and, while displaying customary interest in the opposing ends, kept a sharp watch on the wide holes in the line. What happened was never quite clear to them, for Mt. Millard pulled things off with dazzling speed. The ball shot back from center and well to the left. Some one took it and started to run with it, while the broken line of forwards came together in a moving wall of interference. Alton was not to be held at bay so easily, and she went through. By that time the runner with the ball was well over toward the side-line on his left and when his wall of interference disintegrated he stopped suddenly in his journey, wheeled about and threw the pigskin diagonally across the field to where, lamentably ostracized by Alton, the attenuated full-back was ambling along most unostentatiously. That throw was magnificent both as to distance and accuracy, and it reached the full-back at a moment when the nearest Alton player was a good twenty feet distant. What deserved to be a touchdown, however, resulted in only a seventeen-yard gain, for the full-back, catching close to the side-line, with Slim Staples hard on his heels and Appel coming down on him in front, made the mistake of not edging out into the field while there was still time. The result of this error in tactics was one false step that put a flying foot barely outside the whitewashed streak at the thirty-two yards. I think the referee hated to see that misstep, for if ever a team deserved a touchdown that team was Mt. Millard. Even the Alton stands had to applaud that play.

Mt. Millard went back to regular formation when the ball had been stepped in, and I think Alton breathed easier. The diminutive quarterback used a delayed pass and himself attempted Slim's end and managed to squirm around for three yards. That took the pigskin to Alton's twenty-nine, and with three more downs to draw on there seemed no reason why the visitors shouldn't score a field-goal at least. The Alton stands chanted the "Hold, Alton!" slogan and the visiting contingent shouted loudly and appealingly for a touchdown. The Mt. Millard left half moved back to kicking position and the ball was passed. But, instead of a drop-kick, there was a puzzling double-pass behind the enemy's line and an end, running behind, shot out at the right with the ball snuggled against his stomach and ran wide behind a clever interference to the sixteen yards. Again it was first down, and the enemy had reeled off just fifty-four yards in four plays! It was one of those things that simply couldn't be done—and had been done!

Before Marsh could call his signals again the quarter ended.

CHAPTER XII
VICTORY HARD WON

The long-suffering reader mustn't think that I have any intention of inflicting on him a detailed account of the remaining three periods of that game. I have offended sufficiently already. Besides, it was that first period, with a few moments of the second, and the last quarter only that held the high lights. The in-between was interesting to watch, but it would be dull reading.

Mt. Millard started the second period on Alton's sixteen and, perhaps just to show that she could perform the feat against a still bewildered opponent, slashed a back through between Newton and Renneker for three yards on a fake run around end. Of course had she tried such a thing a second time it wouldn't have come off, but Marsh had no intention of trying it. He deployed his ends, sent his goal-kicker back and then heaved across the center of the line. Fortunately for the defenders of the south goal, Reilly knocked down the ball. After that there wasn't much left for Mt. Millard but a try-at-goal, and after a conference between captain and quarter the try was made. The kicker retreated a good twelve yards from his center, which took him close to the twenty-five line, a retreat that in view of subsequent happenings was well advised. For Alton, stung by recent reverses, piled through the Mt. Millard forwards and hurled aside the guardian backs. It was just those added yards that defeated her. The ball, hurtling away from the kicker's toe, passed safely above upstretched hands and sailed over the cross-bar.

Mt. Millard did a few hand-springs while a 3 was placed to her credit on the score-board, and her delighted supporters yelled themselves hoarse. There was noticeable lack of enthusiasm on the other side of the field, although by the time the opponents again faced each other for the kick-off the Alton cheerers had found their voices again. The balance of the second period held its moments of excitement, but on the whole it was tame and colorless after that first quarter. Alton, regaining the ball after she had kicked it off, started another pilgrimage to the distant goal, smearing the enemy with hard, old-style football and eating up ground steadily if slowly. Once Menge got safely away around the Mt. Millard left end and shot over sixteen yards of trampled turf before an enemy stood him on his head, but for the rest it was gruelling work, the more gruelling as the attack drew near the edge of scoring territory. If Mt. Millard was light of weight she was nevertheless game, and seldom indeed did the Alton attack get started before the enemy was half-way to meet it. Reilly gave place to Kendall in the middle of the journey, and Smedley to Stimson. Mt. Millard likewise called on two fresh recruits to strengthen her line. Alton hammered her way to the Mt. Millard twenty-eight yards and there struck a snag. Greenwood failed to gain at the center, Kendall was repulsed for a slight loss, Greenwood made four on a wide run from kicking position, and then, with seven to gain on fourth down, it was put up to Captain Emerson, and that youth tried hard to tie the score with a placement-kick from just back of the thirty yards. The aim was true enough, but Rus hadn't put quite enough into the swing of his leg and the ball passed just under the bar, so close to it, indeed, that deceived Alton supporters cheered loudly and long before they discovered their error. Mt. Millard kicked on second down and the few plays that brought the half to an end were all in Alton territory.

The visitor presented the same line-up when the third quarter began. For Alton, Red Reilly was back at right half and Garrick was at center in place of Newton. Alton was expected to return refreshed and determined and wreak swift vengeance on the foe, and the anxious cheerers gave the players a fine welcome when they trotted back to the gridiron. But although the Gray-and-Gold seemed to have profited by the interim and played with more skill than before, Mt. Millard was still clever enough to hold her off during the succeeding twelve minutes. Alton tried three forward-passes and made one of them good. This brought a reward of fourteen yards. Another pass grounded and a third went to Mt. Millard. To offset that fourteen yards, the Gray-and-Gold was twice penalized for off-side. Twice Alton reached the enemy's thirty-yard line only to be turned back. The first time Greenwood missed the pass for a six-yard loss and was forced to punt and the other time Mt. Millard intercepted Appel's toss across the left wing. When, at last, the whistle once more sounded, the ball was in Alton's hands close to Mt. Millard's forty-yard line. The teams changed goals and the final period started.

Greenwood got seven yards outside right tackle and put the ball on Mt. Millard's thirty-four. Menge made one through left guard. With two to go, Greenwood smashed through the left of center for six, but the horn sounded and the ball was put back fifteen yards for holding. Greenwood ran from kicking position, but a ubiquitous Mt. Millard end dumped him well back of the line. Greenwood punted to the corner of the field and the ball rolled across the goal-line. Mt. Millard got four yards in two plunges at Stimson and then made the rest of her distance by sending a half around Slim's end. Another attempt at Stimson was good for three yards, but when the full-back tried Renneker he was stopped short. On third down Marsh threw across the field to a waiting half, but Slim knocked the ball aside just short of the receiver's hands. Mt. Millard punted to Alton's twenty-eight and Appel caught and by clever dodging raced back to the forty-one.

Then Alton's big drive began. Using a tackles-back shift, Appel sent Greenwood and Reilly and again Greenwood at the Mt. Millard line, first on one side of center and then on the other, and took the pigskin into the enemy's country. Then Menge got three around left and Slim, running behind, added three more on a wide expedition in the same direction. Greenwood threw short across the center to Captain Emerson, and Rus made five before he was thrown. From the thirty-seven the ball went more slowly, but no less certainly to the twenty-five. There a skin tackle play at the right gained but a yard, and Greenwood again threw forward, the ball grounding. From kick formation Greenwood raced around left for five. With six to go he stood back as if to try a goal, but the ball went to Reilly who, with the right tackle ahead of him, dug a passage through center and made the necessary four yards. After that there was no stopping the invasion. From the fifteen to the four Reilly and Greenwood, alternating, went in four tries. With the Alton stand cheering madly, imploringly, little Menge slid around left end while the attack was faked at the center and made the one-yard. From there Greenwood was pushed over on the second attempt.

When the teams lined up on the five-yard line it was Captain Emerson who went back for the try-at-goal. This time, the line holding stoutly, he had no difficulty in placing the ball over the bar, and it was Alton's turn to celebrate. At last, it seemed, the hoodoo had been broken and Mt. Millard defeated.

There remained, however, more than six minutes of playing time, and much might happen in six minutes. Much did happen, for when, having kicked off to Alton and forced the latter to punt after once gaining her distance, Mt. Millard went back to her bag of tricks. Some of the things she tried were weird and some risky, so risky that only desperation could have counseled them. But too frequently they were successful. A wide formation with both ends on one side of the line and the tackles on the other was good for a twelve-yard gain when the ball was shot obliquely across the field. The runner was spilled before he could get started by Rus Emerson, but twelve yards was enough to move the stakes to a new location. After a plunge at the line, good for two yards, the enemy used the same formation again. But this time a quartering run by a half-back eventuated and was stopped almost at the line. Again Mt. Millard tried a long forward-pass. The receiver was out of position and the ball came back. Faking a punt, the full-back hit the Alton line and went through for eight yards, placing the ball on Alton's forty-six.

Desperately indeed the visitor waged the attack. Mr. Cade sent in three fresh players; Wilde for Stimson, Kerrison for Emerson and Dakin for Reilly. Mt. Millard had already made several substitutions, one a guard who gave Gordon Renneker a hard battle. Forced to punt at last, Mt. Millard sent the ball over the goal-line, and Alton lined up on the twenty. Here it was that Dakin nearly upset the apple-cart. Plunging at tackle on his own side, he let go of the ball, and it trickled across the field with about every warrior after it. It was Slim who finally fell on it on his own eight yards.

Goodwin, standing astride the goal-line, punted on first down, but the ball went high and short, passing out of bounds at the twenty-six, and from there Mt. Millard started again with unabated determination. Greenwood was replaced by Goodwin. A forward-pass made a scant seven yards for the besiegers. Then, from wide-open formation, came another. This time three backs handled the pigskin before it was finally thrown. It would have scored a touchdown had it been caught, but there were two Alton men on the spot, and the Mt. Millard end had no chance. Then the enemy hustled into kick-formation and Alton breathed a sigh of relief. Even if the enemy secured another field-goal the game would still be Alton's. Perhaps Mt. Millard had that knowledge in mind, for she didn't kick, after all. Standing back near the twenty-five-yard streak, Quarterback Marsh poised the ball in the palm of his hand, a tiny motionless figure amidst a maelstrom of rushing forms. Cries of warning filled the air. Marsh, as if unaware of the enemy plunging down on him, surveyed the field. Then, just as Billy Wells bore down with arms upstretched, Marsh side-stepped easily and threw to where, beyond the goal-line, a Mt. Millard end was wheeling into position. Scarcely above the finger-tips of the leaping Alton players sped the oval, fast and straight. The Mt. Millard end ran forward a step, poised for the catch. And then Nemesis in the shape of Slim Staples took a hand. Slim, crashing off a goal-post, staggered into the path of the ball, leaped upward and closed his hands about it. Then he went down into a sea of massing players and a whistle blew shrilly.

The game was over and Alton had won it, 7 to 3. Mt. Millard had staked all on that final play and lost, but there was more honor accruing from that heroic attempt than would have been hers had she secured that field-goal. Defeated but far from disheartened, the tiny quarterback summoned his teammates and cheered heartily if hoarsely for the victors. And Alton, returning the cheer with no more breath than the losers, paid homage to a gallant foe.

Slim emerged from that contest something of a hero and with his right and title to the left end position unassailable. Smedley emerged less fortunately, for he had wrenched a knee so badly that his future use to the team was more than doubtful. There were many other injuries, but none serious. Alton was joyous over having at last won a game from the enemy, but by the next day she was weighing the pros and cons and unwillingly reaching the conclusion that, on the whole, the Gray-and-Gold had a long way to go before she would be in position to face Kenly Hall with better than a one to two chance of winning. There were plenty who stated emphatically that Mt. Millard should have had that game, basing their contention on the more varied and brilliant attack of the visitor. But there were plenty of others who stoutly held that the better team had won, just as the better team does win ninety-nine times in a hundred, and that even allowing Mt. Millard less weight and a far more dazzling and puzzling offense Alton had been there with the good old straight football stuff that wins games. That Mr. Cade was satisfied with the team's showing is very doubtful, but then coaches are like that. They never are satisfied quite. Johnny didn't say anything to lead any one to think he was not content. That was the trouble. He said too little. Those veterans who knew him well understood perfectly that Johnny Cade was not mentally shaking hands with himself!

CHAPTER XIII
AN EVENING CALL

That evening Slim, with his hand prettily painted with iodine, had an engagement that excluded Leonard, and the latter, having no liking for a Saturday evening alone, called up Johnny McGrath on the telephone, found that that youth was to be at home and then walked over to 102 Melrose avenue.

Not only Johnny, but most of Johnny's family was at home, and Leonard was introduced to Mrs. McGrath and Mr. McGrath and young Cullen; Johnny's elder brother was married and lived elsewhere. Leonard liked Mr. and Mrs. McGrath instantly. They were just what they seemed—and vice versa—a thoroughly nice, warm-hearted couple, uncultured but wise and shrewd and well-mannered. Perhaps Leonard took to them the more readily because they made him see at once that they were ready and even anxious to like him. Although Leonard couldn't know it, Johnny had spoken frequently of him, and any one approved of by Johnny was bound to be welcomed by Johnny's parents. And, another thing that Leonard didn't know, even if he suspected it later, very few of Johnny's school acquaintances ever came to his home.

Leonard wasn't filled with instant liking for Cullen, for the younger brother was at the difficult age of thirteen and was long of leg and awkward of speech and movement, a freckle-faced youngster who, knowing of the visitor's connection with the Alton football team, viewed him with piercing intentness and at intervals broke into the general conversation with startlingly inopportune questions. Leonard wasn't quite at his ease until, after a half-hour downstairs, Johnny conveyed him up to his room on the third floor, sternly forbidding the ready Cullen to follow.

That room was quite wonderful, Leonard thought, comparing it to his own small room at home. It was very large, fully twenty feet square, with four big windows framed in gay cretonne and white muslin, two huge closets and book-shelves that went all across one wall. Those shelves made a great hit with the visitor. They were just elbow-high and they had no pesky glass doors in front of them. You could take a book out without the least effort, and you could lay it on top of the shelves and look at it if you didn't want to carry it to a chair. And that was just what Leonard was doing presently. Johnny had more books than the caller had ever seen outside a public library! And such books, too! A full set of the best encyclopedia, all sorts of dictionaries—not only of words, but of places and dates and phrases—and all of Stevenson and Dickens, and Green's and Prescott's histories, and the Badminton Library and lots and lots of other books in sets or single volumes. Leonard thought of his own scanty collection of some two-score tomes—many of them reminders of nursery days—and for a moment was very envious. Then envy passed, and he silently determined to some day have a library as big and complete as Johnny's.

The room was plainly furnished, but everything in it was designed for both comfort and use, a fact that Leonard recognized and that caused him to realize for perhaps the first time that with furniture as with everything else real beauty was founded on usefulness, was intrinsic and not external. Everything in this room was just what it appeared to be. Not a single object masqueraded as something else. Leonard liked it all enormously and said so emphatically, and Johnny was pleased. You could see that.

"I'm glad you like it," he answered almost gratefully. "Dad let me buy everything myself. I could have got stuff that looked a lot—well, a lot grander, do you mind; things with carved legs and all that sort of flummery; but I sort of like plainer things better."

Leonard nodded, looking about the big, pleasantly lighted apartment. "So do I," he agreed, although five minutes ago, had you asked him, he wouldn't have known! "Some room, McGrath," he went on approvingly. "And there's a light just about everywhere, isn't there?"

It did seem so. There was a plain brass standard by the wicker couch, two smaller hood-shaded lights atop the book-shelves, a hanging bulb over the broad chiffonier, a squat lamp on the big, round table and a funny little blue enameled affair on the stand by the head of the bed. Only the table lamp was lighted, but the soft glow radiated to every corner of the room. Leonard's gaze went back to the many shelves opposite.

"Did you buy all those books yourself?" he asked.

"Oh, no, only maybe a third of them. The folks gave me the others. They know I'm fond of them. Joe always gives me books at Christmas and my birthday." He saw the unuttered question in Leonard's face and smiled as he added: "They always ask me what I want, though, first."

Leonard got up then and prowled. He looked at the four pictures in plain dark-oak frames: "The Retreat from Moscow"; a quaint print of an elderly man standing before a second-hand bookstall on a Paris quay holding a huge umbrella overhead while, with one volume tucked under an arm, he peered near-sightedly into a second; a photograph of Hadrian's Tomb and a Dutch etching of a whirling windmill, with bent sedges about a little pool and an old woman bending against the wind.

"I like that one a lot," explained Johnny. "Can't you just see—no, I mean feel the wind? I'd like to go to Holland some day. It must be fine, I'm thinking."

Leonard had a go at the books next, Johnny pulling forth his special treasures for him. After awhile they sat down again and talked, and when, as was to be expected, football came up for discussion, the discussion became animated. Although Johnny didn't play, he was a keen critic—and a fearless one. "There's two or three fellows on the team," he declared after the day's contest had been gone over, "that would be better for a vacation, to my mind. Put them on the bench for a week, maybe, and they'd come back and earn their keep."

Leonard wanted to know the names of the gentlemen, but wasn't sure he ought to ask. Johnny supplied them, however, without urging. "It's Smedley and Garrick and that big Renneker I'm thinking of," he explained. "Take Smedley, now, sure he's a good man, but he don't ever spit on his hands and get to work, Grant. It's the same way with the other two, especially Renneker. He's asleep at the switch half the time."

"But I thought he played a pretty good game to-day," objected Leonard.

94

"He did, but what's a 'pretty good game' for a fellow who's made the All-Scholastic?" asked Johnny witheringly. "Sure, 'tis no game at all. He has the height of a camel and the weight of a whale, and does he use either intelligently? He does not! I'm no football player, Grant—or should I be calling you General?—but I can see with half an eye, and that one shut, that the lad isn't earning his salary."

"He doesn't get any," laughed Leonard.

"I know, that was a figure of speech," answered the other. "Though, by the same token, I'll bet he'd take the salary if it was offered."

"You mean—" Leonard stopped. Then he added: "Slim thinks you maybe made a mistake about Renneker that time."

"I thought so myself," responded Johnny. "But this afternoon I got Jimsy Carnochan to go to the game with me. Mind you, I said no word to him about Renneker or Ralston or any one else. I just wanted to see would he notice anything. Well, in the third quarter, when the play was close to where we were sitting, Jimsy said to me, 'Who's the big fellow there playing right guard?' 'On which team?' I asked him. 'On Alton.' 'His name's Gordon Renneker.' 'Like fun,' said Jimsy. 'If it is my name's Napoleon Bonaparte! Don't you mind the fellow that played first base in New Haven last summer for the Maple Leaf team? I've forgotten his name, but 'twill come to me.' 'Ralston, do you mean?' I asked him. 'Ralston! That's the guy! What's he calling himself out of his name for now?' 'Sure,' I said, 'you're mistaken. There's a similarity, I'll acknowledge, but this fellow is Gordon Renneker, a fine lad that got placed on the All-Scholastic Team last year.' 'Maybe he was placed on it, whatever it is,' said Jimsy, 'and he's likewise placed in my memory, for the big piece of cheese caught me with my foot off the bag, and I'm not forgetting any guy that does that!' Well, I told him that he couldn't be certain, seeing that you're always reading about people that look so much alike their own mothers can't tell them apart, maybe; and I minded him of a moving picture play that was here no longer ago than last August where one man takes another man's place in Parliament and no one knows any different. And finally I said to him: 'Whatever you may be thinking, Jimsy, keep it to yourself, for if it turned out that you were mistaken you'd feel mighty small, what with getting an innocent fellow into trouble.' So there's no fear of Jimsy talking, General."

Leonard looked perplexed. "It's awfully funny," he said finally. "Renneker isn't at all the sort of fellow you'd think to find playing baseball for money. Look at the clothes he wears, and—and the impression he gives you. Why, he must have plenty of money, McGrath."

"You'd think so. Still, I mind the time when I had all the good clothes I could get on my back and would have been glad of the chance of picking up a bit of money. Although," added Johnny, "I don't think I'd change my name to do it."

"Well," said Leonard, shaking his head in puzzlement, "I can't get it. What's troubling me, though, is this. Knowing what we do—or suspecting it, rather—ought we to tell some one? I mean Coach Cade or Rus Emerson or faculty."

"I'm wondering that myself," said Johnny, frowning. "Maybe it's no business of mine, though, for I'm not connected with football—"

"What difference does that make?" Leonard demanded. "You're an Alton fellow, aren't you? If what you suspect about Gordon Renneker is true he ought not to be allowed to play for Alton, and as an Alton student—"

"Sure, that's true enough," agreed Johnny ruefully. "I was fearing you'd say that. I've said it to myself already." He grinned across at his guest. After a moment he continued: "There's this about it, though, General. I've no proof, no real proof, I mean. Like I told Jimsy Carnochan, it might be I was mislead by one of those strange resemblances that you read of."

"Yes," answered Leonard without conviction. "You might be. I guess you'll just have to do as you think best."

Johnny's eyes twinkled. "Sure, and how about you?" he asked innocently.

"Me?"

"Yes, for I've told you all there is to be told. How about you speaking of it to the coach or some one?"

"Gee, I couldn't!" Leonard protested. "I'm playing on the team, or, anyway, the squad, and it wouldn't look very well for me to—to prefer charges against another member, now would it?"

Johnny laughed merrily. "I can't do it because I'm not on the team, and you can't do it because you are!" Then he sobered. "We'll leave it as it is," he decided. "I want to do what's right, but I don't know that it would be right to accuse Renneker of this with no real proof to back up the charge with. Besides, if he plays no better game than he's been playing, 'twill work no injustice to the teams we meet, for, with him out of it, the coach might put in a fellow that would be a sight better."

"Do you think I'd better say anything to Slim about what happened to-day?" asked Leonard.

"I wouldn't," said Johnny dryly. "'Twould only worry him. Slim's all for sticking his head in the sand, like an ostrich, and there's no call to be twitching his tail-feathers!"

Leonard had to laugh at that, and no more was said on the subject that evening. In fact, the evening was about gone. At the front door, Johnny, bidding the caller "Good night," added a bit wistfully: "'Twas fine of you to come and see me, Grant, and I appreciate it. I'd be liking it if you'd come again some time."

"Why, I liked it myself," laughed Leonard from the steps. "And I surely will come again. And, say, why don't you ever come and see Slim and me?"

"Well, I don't know," answered Johnny. "Maybe I might some time."

"I wish you would," Leonard assured him. "We're almost always at home evenings."

Going on down the hill, Leonard reflected that the probable reason why Johnny had never called at Number 12 Haylow was that he had never been asked.

The doors were still open when Leonard reached Haylow, but ten o'clock struck just as he was climbing the stairs. In Number 12 the light was burning and in the bed at the left Slim was fast asleep, a magazine spread open across his chest. Leonard set about preparing for slumber with stealthy movements. Perhaps he need not have taken so much trouble, though, for when he inadvertently knocked a French dictionary from the corner of the table and it fell with a slam loud enough to make him jump an inch off the floor Slim didn't even stir. It was not until Leonard was in his pajamas that his gaze happened on a half-sheet of paper pinned squarely in the middle of his pillow. He held it to the light and read:

"If I'm asleep when you return
  Then wake me up, I pray,
 For there is something that I yearn
  2 you 2 night 2 say."

Leonard smiled and turned doubtfully toward the sleeper. It seemed too bad to awaken him. Whatever it was that he had to tell could doubtless wait for morning. Still, Slim never had any trouble getting to sleep, and so—

"Wake up, Slim!" Leonard shook him gently. Slim slumbered on. "*Slim!* Here, snap out of it! *Hi, Slim!*" Slim muttered and strove to slip away from the rough, disturbing grasp. "No, you don't! You wanted to be waked up, and I'm going"—shake—"to wake you up"—shake—"if it takes all night!" Slim opened his eyes half an inch and observed Leonard with mild interest. Then:

"That you, General?" he muttered.

"Yes."

"Good night."

"Hold on! What was it you wanted to say to me, you silly coot?"

"Huh?"

"Come awake a minute. You left a note on my pillow—something you wanted to say to me—remember?"

"Yes," answered Slim sleepily.

"Well, say it then!"

"I did. That was it."

"What was it?"

"'Good night.'"

Slim turned his back and pulled the clothes up over his ears.

CHAPTER XIV
MR. CADE MAKES AN ENTRY

The next afternoon when Leonard clumped down the steps of the gymnasium clad for practice a gust of cold air swept around the corner from the north-west and reminded him that November was two days old. The sky was gray and clouds sailed low overhead. Fallen leaves played prankishly along the walks and eddied into quiet harbors about the buildings. After the warm, moist air of the locker room the outdoor world felt chill indeed, and Leonard, trudging briskly toward the gridiron, rolled his hands in the edge of his old sweater. It was a day, though, that made the blood move fast and called for action. Leonard, to use his own phrase, felt full of "pep." They couldn't work a fellow too hard or too fast on such an afternoon.

Practice went off at a new gait, and when, routine work over, those who had played through Saturday's game were released and Mr. Fadden's charges romped over from the second team gridiron, every one knew that fur was going to fly. And fly it did. A fellow had to work and keep on working just to be comfortably warm, but besides that there was a quality in the harshly chill wind that would have made an oyster ambitious and put speed into a snail. The second started in with lots of ginger and smeared up Carpenter's run-back of the kick-off, and after that held the first and made her punt from her twenty-two yards. After that it was hammer-and-tongs, the rival coaches barking out directions and criticisms and hopping about on the edge of the scrap in the most absorbed way. If every one hadn't been too much interested with the battle the spectacle of Mr. Fadden hopping might have occasioned amusement!

The first presented a line-up of substitutes, with Gurley and Kerrison playing end, Lawrence and Cash tackle, Squibbs and Falls guard, Muller center, Carpenter quarter, Kendall and Goodwin half and Dakin full. Leonard, huddled in a blanket on the bench, forgot the cold in the cheering knowledge that sooner or later Johnny Cade would be sure to call on him. Johnny Cade did, but not until the second period. Meanwhile Lawrence and Cash took plenty of punishment from the cocky scrubs but managed to hold out. Second was certainly on her toes this afternoon, and nothing the first could do prevented her from scoring. It was only a field-goal, for the first, pushed down the field to her twenty-yard line, held gamely through three downs, but it meant three points for the scrubs and much exulting. With a strong wind almost behind him, the second's left half could hardly have failed to boot the pigskin over.

First wrested the ball away from second a minute or so later and started a march toward the opponent's goal. Kendall got away with a nice run of a dozen yards, and Dakin twice got half that distance through left guard. Goodwin plugged hard, but it was not his day. Carpenter tried a quarterback run and made it good for eight yards, placing the ball on second's twenty-four. Kendall went back and faked a try-at-goal, taking the pigskin on a wide end run that netted him little but exercise. Then a forward-pass was tried, but, short as it was, the wind bore it down, and first was lucky not to lose possession of it. With two downs left, Kendall again threatened a field-goal, but passed the ball to Dakin, and the full-back smashed through the enemy left for four. On the same play Dakin added enough to make it first down on the fourteen. Then, with first already tasting success, the whistle ended the period!

The scrubs crossed the field to sit in a closely huddled group like a lot of blanketed Indians and Leonard watched Mr. Cade hopefully. But when the second period started the coach made but two changes in his line-up. Raleigh went in at right guard and Wilde at right tackle. Leonard, disappointed, looked searchingly up and down the bench. So far as he knew he was the only tackle remaining. In fact, only less than a dozen fellows were left now, and he didn't think there was a lineman among them. He didn't wish Lawrence any bad luck, but it did seem that he had played about long enough!

First had a streak of luck right at the start of that period, for a second team back fumbled on his forty-four and, although second recovered the ball, the next line-up was close to the twenty-five-yard line. Two punches and then a punt into the gale that carried a scant twenty yards, and the ball was first's in scrub territory. The first attack sent Goodwin at the enemy's center for a two-yard gain and when the warriors had disentangled themselves one form remained on the ground. Jake seized water bottle and sponge and trotted out. "That's Raleigh," said the fellow at Leonard's right.

"Sure?" asked Leonard anxiously. "I thought maybe it was Lawrence. No, there's Lawrence. You a guard?"

The neighbor shook his head sadly. "Half," he answered.

They had Raleigh standing up now and Jake was leading him toward the bench. Coach Cade's voice came imperatively.

"First team guard!" he called.

The trainer echoed the summons impatiently as he neared the bench. "Come on, one of you guards!"

Leonard threw off his blanket and bent mutely to the neighbor and the substitute halfback seized his sweater while Leonard pulled himself out of it. Then he dashed onto the gridiron. Jake was a dozen feet away, still supporting the scowling Raleigh.

"What's the matter?" he asked. "Deaf? Didn't you hear the coach yelling?" Then he stared harder, at Leonard's back now, and called suddenly: "Here! You ain't a guard!"

But Leonard paid no heed. Perhaps the wind bore the words away from him. He went on, aware, as he gained the waiting squad, of the coach's puzzled gaze.

"I called for a guard, Grant," said Mr. Cade.

"Yes, sir," answered Leonard. "I've played guard two seasons."

"Maybe, but you're not a guard now. Send some one else on. Isn't there any one there?"

"No, sir."

Mr. Cade shrugged. "All right. You take it then. You deserve it, I'm blessed if you don't! Come on now, First Team! Let's get going! All right, Quarter!"

Leonard stepped in between Garrick and Cash, Carpenter chanted his signal and the lines ground together. Why, this was easy, reflected Leonard. It was just like old times. He knew what to do here. When you were a guard you were a guard and nothing else.

You didn't have to understudy your next door neighbor and go prancing around like a silly end! Of course, when a shift took you around to the other side of the line, as it was doing now —

Leonard whanged into an opponent and tipped him neatly aside as Kendall came spinning through. Three yards, easy. Maybe four. This was "pie!" He got back to his place again and grinned at his second team adversary. The scrub player answered the grin with a malignant scowl. Leonard laughed to himself. He always liked the other fellow to get good and peeved; that made it easier. Dakin was stopped short on the next play and Kendall went back. A second team back tried to sneak inside of Leonard, and Leonard gave him a welcoming shoulder. Then there was the thud of the ball and he pushed an adversary aside and sped down the field, the gale behind him helping him on. He was under the ball all the way and was hard by when Kerrison upset the scrub quarter for no gain. The pigskin was on the second's fourteen now, and the second realized its difficulties. Kicking into that wind was a thankless job. If you kicked low your ends couldn't cover the punt. If you kicked high you made no distance. Even a forward-pass, were you rash enough to attempt it under your own goal-posts, was doubly risky. So second tried hard to get a half-back around an end, first at Gurley's post and then at Kerrison's, and made but four yards altogether. It seemed then that second must punt, but she had one more trick up her sleeve. She sent an end far out to the left, shifted to the right and sent the full-back straight ahead. Well, that wasn't so bad, for it added another four yards to her total. But it was fourth down, and the wind still blew hard against her, and punt she must at last. So punt she tried to.

That she didn't was primarily due to the ease with which Leonard disposed of his man and went romping through the scrub line, quite alone for the instant. A half met him, and the impact, since Leonard had his hands thrown high, almost drove the breath from his body. Yet the damage was done, for the second team kicker was too hurried to punt. Instead, he tucked the ball to his elbow and shot off to the right in a desperate attempt to circle the first team's end. But there was Gurley to be considered, and Gurley dropped his man very expeditiously and neatly for a six-yard loss. Whereupon first took the ball, lined up on the scrub's sixteen and hammered Goodwin and Dakin over for the score.

Then Kendall booted a nice goal and made it seven points, and going back up the field Carpenter and Dakin and half a dozen others whacked Leonard on the back and pantingly told him that he was "all right," or words to that effect. Then first kicked off again and went after another touchdown. You might criticize the second's science, but you had to acknowledge that when it came to fight she was right on hand! Second didn't hold with Mr. Cade or Quarterback Carpenter when they assured the first that there was another score to be had. Second denied it loudly and with ridicule. She dared first to try to get another score. First accepted the challenge with ejaculations of derision and the trouble began again.

You mustn't think that Leonard played through some ten minutes without receiving his share of censure from the coach and the quarterback, for nothing like that happened. Mr. Cade showed little partiality, and every one came in for criticism or rebuke. What Carpenter said worried Leonard very little. Quarterbacks are always nagging a fellow. But he did wish, toward the last, that Mr. Cade would stop barking at him. Of course he knew that he didn't play the position perfectly, but he was doing his best, gosh ding it, and no one was making any gains through him! If only he was a little bigger and had more beef he'd show Johnny some real playing!

As it was, though, he was doing so well that the coach was secretly marvelling. Mr. Cade viewed Leonard's height and his none too broad shoulders and then glanced at the big Garrick on one side and the rangy Cash on the other and wondered. "When," reflected the coach, "he told me he was a guard he knew what he was talking about!" Much of Leonard's success this afternoon was due to following Billy Wells' advice. Leonard looked his man in the eye and discovered that, in some strange fashion, he could tell what the chap was going to do a fraction of a second before he started to do it. It was almost like mind-reading, Leonard thought. And he profited, too, by the other tips that Billy had given him. He couldn't adopt Billy's stance thoroughly, but he did try a modified form of it and found that it gave him a quicker start. And to-day no one drove his head back and made him see whole constellations of wonderful stars! No, sir, the old chin was right in against the neck!

First didn't succeed in scoring again, but she did throw a scare into the adversary in the final minute of play. By that time Leonard's original opponent had been replaced by a fresher but, as it was soon proved, no more formidable youth, and Mr. Fadden had made other substitutions in his array of talent. So, too, had Mr. Cade, although the latter's resources were nearly exhausted. Cruikshank went in for Carpenter, and a new half-back appeared. Cruikshank brought a little more "pep" to the first, and she got the pigskin down to second's twenty-eight yards. There, however, the enemy stiffened and tightened and took the ball away on downs. Wisely, she elected to punt on first down, but there was a poor pass, and the ball was missed entirely by the kicker. It hit him somewhere around the feet and bounded to one side. Instantly twenty-two youths made for it. Some four or five reached it more or less simultaneously. Of the number was the first team right guard. How that happened was a subject of official investigation later by Mr. Fadden. However, the second team's troubles are not ours. What interests us is the fact that not only was Leonard the first man through the second team line but he was the first man to lay hand on the ball. He accomplished the latter feat by diving between two hesitant adversaries and, being doubtless favored by luck, capturing the erratic pigskin during one brief instant of quiescence. A fraction of a second later that ball would have toppled this way or that, or jumped into the air, eluding Leonard's grasp just as it had eluded others', but at the instant it had presumably paused for breath. Anyhow, Leonard reached it and pulled it under him and tucked his head out of the way. Then half a dozen of the opponents sat on him more or less violently or tried to get covetous hands on the prize. The whistle blew and finally he breathed again. Having been pulled to his feet, his breathing was again disturbed by emphatic blows on his back or shoulders accompanied by brief but hearty expression of commendation. He was still fighting for breath when Cruikshank piped his signal, and Dakin drove harmlessly into the second team line. Then, to the intense disgust of the first and the vast relief of the second, with the ball on the seventeen yards and a score as sure as shooting, some idiot blew a whistle!

There was almost a scrap about that. Up in the locker room Dakin accused Winship, the assistant manager who had acted as timekeeper, of having cheated the first of a score. "Time," answered Winship coldly, "was up when the whistle blew." "Yah," responded Dakin impolitely. "You're crazy! You didn't see straight! Bet you there was a good thirty seconds left!" "There was not! If anything, you had a second more than was coming to you, for the whistle didn't blow until I'd called to Tenney twice. No use being sore at me, Dakin. Much better have done something when you had the ball that time!" "Is that so?" snarled the full-back. "How'd I know you were going to cheat us out of—" "Don't you say I cheated!" "Well, what do you call it, you fathead? Step up to the gym with me if you're looking for trouble!"

But some of the others stepped in just there, and hostilities were prevented, and somewhat later Dakin, having been cooled by an icy shower-bath, apologized handsomely and the entente cordiale was reëstablished.

That evening, his briar pipe drawing nicely and his feet comfortably elevated, Coach Cade turned the pages of his little memorandum book and made marks here and there. Once he reversed his pencil and, using the rubber-tipped end of it, expunged a name entirely. The last thing he did was to draw a black mark through the words "Grant, Leonard" and through half a dozen mysterious hieroglyphics that followed them and then, turning a page, enter the same words again very carefully in his small characters. At the top of the latter page was the inscription "Guards."

CHAPTER XV
A TIP FROM MCGRATH

Leonard regretted that Slim hadn't been at the field during scrimmage that afternoon, for he wanted Slim to know that he had — well, done not so badly. All he told the other, though, when they met before supper was that Johnny had run out of guards and that he had played at right for awhile.

"Guard?" said Slim in surprise. "You mean Johnny stood for it?" Slim frowned. "Look here, General, let me give you a word of advice. You never get anywhere by changing jobs. You stick to being a tackle. The next time Johnny wants to shift you to some other position you put your foot down."

"It wasn't Johnny did it, Slim. They yelled for a guard and I ran on."

"More fool you, son. You've got to specialize, or you'll just sit on the bench forever and ever. The fellow that does a little of everything never does much of anything, as some one once very wisely remarked. How did you get along?"

"All right," answered Leonard. "It was easier than tackle, Slim. I—I was more at home there, I suppose."

"Huh," grumbled Slim, "don't get to looking for the easy jobs, General. You stay put, young feller. Why, only a couple of days ago Billy Wells was telling me what a wonderful tackle you'd make!"

"Wells was?" exclaimed Leonard. "Get out, Slim!"

"He was, honest to goodness! Why, Billy's a—a great admirer of yours, General. He said more nice things about your playing than I ever heard him say about any fellow's—not excepting his own! And now you go and let them make a goat of you. Too bad, son."

"We-ell, I've half a notion that Johnny will let me play guard after this," said Leonard. It was more a hope than a notion, though. Slim shook his head doubtfully.

"I wouldn't bank on it," he said. "You know, General, you aren't quite built for a guard."

After supper—Slim had been eating at training table for a long while now—Leonard was leaning over a Latin book in Number 12 when the door opened violently and things began to happen to him. First he was precipitated backward until his head touched the floor and his feet gyrated in air. Then he was sat on while rude hands tweaked his nose and the lately occupied chair entangled his feet. About that time Leonard began to resent the treatment and got a firm hold on Slim's hair. But Slim wouldn't have that.

"No, General," he announced firmly. "Be quiet and take your medicine. You are being disciplined, son. This isn't a mere vulgar brawl. This is for the good of your poor little shriveled soul."

"Well, let up on my nose then, you crazy idiot! What am I being disciplined for! And get off my tummy a minute so I can kick that blamed chair out of the way!"

"Don't vent your spleen on the poor inanimate chair," remonstrated Slim reproachfully. "It never did anything to you, you deceiving goof. Look at me! In the eye—I mean eyes! Why didn't you tell me what happened this afternoon?"

"I did."

"General!"

"Ouch! Quit, you—you crazy—"

"Why didn't you tell me *all*? Look at me, consarn yer!"

"I am, Slim! Doggone it, will you quit?"

"Stop struggling! General, you've got to come clean. Did you or didn't you deceive me?"

"I did not."

"General, you did. Since then I have learned the truth. You went and made yourself one of these here football heroes, you did, General. Broke through—no, crashed through the enemy line and fell on the fumbled ball, thus bringing victory to your beloved Alma Mater! Not once, but twice did you do this thing. I know all, and lying won't help you any longer. Confess, drat your pesky hide! Did you or isn't they?"

"They is!" groaned Leonard. "For the love of Mike, Slim, get off my supper!"

Slim removed himself, and Leonard struggled out of the clutches of the chair and got to his feet. "For two cents," he said, "I'd lay you over that blamed chair and paddle you, Slim."

"No, you wouldn't, son. You know very well that you deserved all you got, and a little bit more. You deceived me, me your friend! You—"

"Oh, dry up," laughed Leonard. "What did you expect me to do? Tell you how good I was? Those second team fellows that played against me were dead easy, Slim. A child could have got through those chaps. Why, you could yourself, Slim! Well, I won't go that far, but—"

"I pay no heed to your insults, you gallery-player!"

"Shut up! There wasn't any gallery to-day. It was too cold."

"Gallery enough. Fellows at table spent about half the time talking about you and your stunts. And I had to make believe I knew all about it and keep nosing around for clews. Not for worlds would I have confessed that I knew naught of which they spake. Fancy my position! Me who raised you from a cradle! Aren't you ashamed of yourself?"

"Awfully," said Leonard. "Now will you dry up and let me get this Latin?"

"I will not. Say, General, I wish you'd set to work and get Renneker's job away from him."

"That's likely," scoffed Leonard. "What you got against Renneker?"

"Nothing. Only—" Slim sobered, and after a moment's pause continued: "Only that yarn of Johnny McGrath's makes me sort of wonder whether—well, if Renneker wasn't on the team, General, there wouldn't be anything to worry about!"

"I thought you'd decided that there wasn't anything in that idea of McGrath's."

"So I had. I'm still that way. Only—well, I wish some one would find out the truth of it. Or you'd beat him out for the place!"

"I've got a fine chance, Slim! Look here, if you think there's a chance that McGrath isn't mistaken why don't you ask Renneker about it?"

Slim shrugged. "It isn't my funeral. Besides, what's to prevent him from lying?"

Leonard shook his head. "I don't believe he would, Slim. He doesn't seem that sort, you know."

"No," agreed Slim, grudgingly, "he doesn't. Oh, well, I should worry. Gee, I've got enough to attend to without turning reformer. There's the class dinner Saturday, and Cash tells me only about half the bunch have paid up so far. By the way, have you heard anything?"

"Not a thing," replied Leonard.

"Guess you haven't tried very hard," grumbled the other. "I'd like to know what the freshies are up to. They've got something planned. You can see that by the knowing look of 'em. Some fool stunt the juniors have put 'em up to, I'll wager. Well—"

Slim relapsed into thoughtful silence, and Leonard edged his chair back to the table. After a minute he asked: "That all?"

"Huh?" inquired Slim absently.

"If you're quite through I'll have another go at this Latin," said Leonard politely. "But of course if there's anything else on your mind—"

"Go to the dickens," growled Slim.

On Tuesday the first-string players returned to a full diet of work and, excepting Smedley, now pronounced out of football for the season, all the guard candidates were on hand when the scrimmage started. Nevertheless Leonard displaced Renneker in the second period and Raleigh went in at left guard, relieving Stimson. Billy Wells greeted Leonard heartily with a playful poke in the ribs and, "Well, here's the General! See who's with us, Jim!" Jim Newton turned and grinned. "Hello, sonny," he said. "You get behind me and they won't hurt you." Leonard, almost painfully aware of the difference in size between him and the big center, smiled apologetically. "Thanks," he answered, "I will if you happen to be on your feet." Billy yelped gleefully, and Jim's grin broadened. "You win, young feller," he said.

Leonard didn't break through to-day and capture a fumbled ball, but he did more than handle his opponent and very early in the second period the scrubs discovered that the right of the first team line was a particularly poor place at which to direct attack. Leonard and Wells worked together very nicely. Just before the end, much to his disgust, he was forced to yield his place to Falls, and he and Raleigh, also relieved, made their way back to the gymnasium together. Raleigh was an excellent example of the player who is able to progress just so far and then stands still, in spite of all that coaches can do. He had been a second-string guard last year and had, early in the present season, been picked as a certainty. Renneker's advent, however, had spoiled his chance, and since then Raleigh seemed to have lost his grip. Just now he was not so much standing still as he was sliding backward. He confided something of this to Leonard on the way across to the gymnasium.

"I don't suppose I'll even get a smell of the big game," he said sorrowfully. "Renneker'll play at right and Stimson at left, and you and Falls will be next choice. It was that big guy that queered my chances."

Leonard didn't have to ask who was meant. Instead he said comfortingly: "You can't tell, Raleigh. You might beat Stimson yet. And you'll surely have it all over me for first substitute."

But Raleigh shook his head. "Not a chance, Grant. I know a real player when I see him, even if I'm getting to be a dub myself. You're a live-wire. I wouldn't be surprised if you got Stimson's job before the Kenly game."

"Me? Much obliged for the compliment, Raleigh, but I guess Stimson isn't frightened much! I haven't got the weight, you know."

"You don't seem to need it," replied Raleigh enviously. "You've got speed to burn. Wish I had a little of it!"

The next day Leonard was called to the training table, where he took his place between Lawrence and Wilde and where, after his second or third repast, he was no longer Grant but "General." On Wednesday he discovered with something of a thrill that Coach Cade was taking him seriously as a candidate for a guard position, for he was given a hard thirty-minute drill in blocking and breaking through in company with Renneker and Stimson and Raleigh and Falls. Soon after that, just when Leonard didn't know, Squibbs disappeared from the football squad. It will be remembered, perhaps, that not long before Coach Cade had erased a name from a page of his little book.

It was on Thursday evening that Johnny McGrath appeared at Number 12 Haylow in response to Leonard's invitation. Both Leonard and Slim were at home, and Johnny had no cause to doubt that he was welcome. The conversation was not particularly interesting. Or, at least, it wouldn't sound so if set down here. There was one subject not included in the many that were discussed, and that was the resemblance of Gordon Renneker to George Ralston. Just before he left Johnny said, a trifle hesitantly: "By the way, Slim, heard anything about Saturday?"

"About the dinner, do you mean?" Slim's eyes narrowed.

"Yes. I wondered if you'd heard any—er—any rumors." Johnny looked very innocent just then. Slim shook his head slowly.

"Nothing much, Johnny. Have you?"

"Why, I don't know." Johnny appeared undecided. "You see, I'm a junior, Slim, and maybe I oughtn't to give away any freshman secrets."

"Huh," Slim grumbled, "if it wasn't for you fellows putting 'em up to the mischief—"

"Sure, I had nothing to do with it," laughed Johnny. "And what I heard didn't come from my crowd. 'Tis just something I accidentally came on."

"Well, out with it. What are the pesky kids up to?"

"I'm not knowing that, Slim."

"Well, what the dickens do you know, you Sinn Feiner?"

"All I know," replied Johnny evasively, as he opened the door, "is that if I was President of the Sophomore Class I'd be watching out mighty sharp come Saturday evening." Johnny grinned, winked meaningly and vanished.

"Humph," said Slim. "He does know something, the silly ass." He started up as if to go after Johnny, but then sat down again and shrugged his shoulders. "He wouldn't tell, I suppose."

"What do you think he was hinting at?" asked Leonard.

Slim shrugged again. "How the dickens do I know? I dare say the freshies have cooked up some plot to make me look silly. Maybe they think they can keep me away from the dinner. All right, let them try it!" And Slim looked grim as he began to disrobe.

On Saturday Leonard made his first trip away from Alton with the football team, being one of twenty-six fellows who journeyed to New Falmouth. Last fall Alton had just managed to defeat the clever High School team by one point, and to-day the visitors weren't looking for any easy victory. It was well they weren't, as events proved. New Falmouth was too powerful for the Gray-and-Gold. With only one more game on her schedule, and that against a rival high school of smaller calibre, New Falmouth was in position to use everything she had in to-day's contest. And she certainly held nothing back. Last season's game, lost to her through her inability to convert two touchdowns into goals, had been a disappointment, and she fully intended to take her revenge.

Coach Cade started with several substitutes in his line-up, but this was not because he held the enemy in contempt. His real reason was that he hoped to hold New Falmouth scoreless in the first half of the game and use his best talent to tuck the victory away in the last. But that wasn't to be. Before the second quarter was half-way through Johnny Cade was hurling his best troops onto the field in a desperate attempt to turn the tide of battle. For by that time New Falmouth had scored twice and had 10 points to her credit on the score-board while the visitors had yet to show themselves dangerous.

Leonard didn't see service until the third period. Then he went in at left guard in place of the deposed Stimson. The score was still 10 to 0, and Alton looked very much like a beaten team. New Falmouth had a powerful attack, one that was fast and shifty and hit hard. No place in the Gray-and-Gold line had proved invulnerable in the first two periods, while the home team had run the ends with alarming frequency. Only Alton's ability to pull herself together and stand firm under her goal had prevented the enemy's score from being doubled.

Leonard had Jim Newton on one side of him and Sam Butler on the other when the second half began. He had not played beside Butler before and didn't know the tall youth's style of game as well as he knew Billy Wells', and for awhile the two didn't work together any too smoothly. In fact, the left of the Alton line was no more difficult to penetrate than the right until Leonard discovered from experience that Butler went about his business in a different fashion from that used by Billy and began to govern his own play accordingly. Butler couldn't be depended on, for one thing, to back up attacks between left guard and center. Such plays always pulled him in and left him fairly useless. Also, he played too high much of the time, a fact that invited more attacks at his position than Leonard approved of. Yet, when once these facts had been learned, Leonard was able to discount them to an appreciable extent and before the third period was more than half over New Falmouth was less attentive to that side of the adversary's line.

Leonard knew that he was playing football, and extremely hard football, before the third play had been made. New Falmouth got the ball on the kick-off and started a battering-ram attack that bore the enemy back time and again. Leonard went through some punishment then, for the first three plays were aimed at the Alton left guard and tackle. He acquired a bleeding nose in the second of them and a bruised knee in the third. About that time he got interested and began to really fight. Captain Emerson went off with a bad limp and Kerrison took his place. Not much later Bee Appel, after having been aimed at since the game began, was finally downed for good and Carpenter took over the running of the team.

The third period ended without further scoring, although the ball had stayed in Alton territory most of the time and was still there.

A penalty for off-side set Alton back another five yards nearer her goal just after play was resumed, and, when she had been held for two downs on the twenty-two yards, New Falmouth tried a goal from placement. For once, however, the line failed to hold and half the Alton team piled through on the kicker and the ball bounded off up the field and was captured by Reilly, of Alton, on the thirty-six yards. Alton made first down on two plunges and a six-yard run by Menge. Then, however, after three more attempts, Greenwood punted to the home team's twenty-five, where the ball went outside. New Falmouth made two through Renneker and tore off five more around Kerrison. A third down was wasted on a plunge at center that was repulsed. Then New Falmouth tried her third forward-pass of the game, and the ball landed nicely in the hands of Slim Staples close to the forty-yard line, and Slim dodged to the thirty-two before he was stopped.

Here, it seemed, was Alton's chance to score at last, but after Carpenter had attempted a run following a delayed pass and had centered the ball at the sacrifice of a yard, the chance didn't look so bright. Greenwood made a scant two at the New Falmouth left, and then, with nine to go on third down, and Greenwood in kicking position, Carpenter called for an end-around play with Slim Staples carrying. Just what happened Leonard didn't know, but somewhere between Jim Newton and Slim the ball got away. Leonard heard Carpenter's frantic grunt of *"Ball!"* and swung into the enemy. Then he felt the ball trickle against his foot, thrust aside for a moment and dropped to a knee. When he got his hands on the pigskin the battle was all about him, and cries and confusion filled the air. Yet he was able to thrust himself up again through the mêlée, and plunge forward, and, having taken that first plunge, to go on. He met a back squarely and caromed off him into the arms of another, broke loose somehow and went forward again. The goal-line was startlingly near, and he made for it desperately, slanting first to the left and then doubling back from a frenzied quarter. He and the quarter met and, spinning on a heel, he staggered over the line, a New Falmouth man astride him as he fell.

Unfortunately there was no one left on the Alton team who could kick a goal once in five times, and Joe Greenwood, who tried to add another point to the six, failed dismally. The fault wasn't entirely his, though, for New Falmouth broke through and hurried the kick. But even to have scored was something, and Leonard, still wondering just how it had happened, was appraised of the fact in most emphatic language and actions. Over on one side of the field a half-hundred or so of Alton sympathizers who had accompanied the eleven were shouting ecstatically and wildly. Denied victory, they made much of that touchdown.

The ball went to New Falmouth for the kick-off, and Leonard sprang away to repel the invaders. Behind him, Carpenter got the pigskin, juggled it and tried to run it back, but two New Falmouth ends downed him fiercely. On the second play Greenwood got clean away around the left end and made it first down on the thirty-yard line. Just as he was jubilating hoarsely over that Leo Falls came romping on, hailed the referee and joyfully slapped Leonard on the back.

"You're off," he announced. "Let's have your head-guard."

Leonard looked unbelievingly at him. "Off?" he gasped. "Me?" But the referee was waving impatiently, and Leonard pulled off his helmet and turned sadly toward the bench. The world seemed just then filled with ingratitude and injustice, and the cheer that hailed him fell on unresponsive ears. Jake hurried out to enfold him in a blanket, mumbling fine phrases, and Mr. Cade said something as Leonard passed to the bench, but the day's hero was not to be salved so easily. From the bench he sadly watched the game to its end and witnessed, in the closing moments, the addition of another 3 to New Falmouth's 10. Life was very dark!

CHAPTER XVI
FIRST TRICK TO THE ENEMY

But time heals all wounds, and long before the special trolley had landed the team back at Alton Leonard's spirits were again at normal, or perhaps a little beyond normal since, in spite of the defeat, the Gray-and-Gold had had her big moments, and he had shared in at least one of them. Disappointment had not prevented the other members of the squad from giving praise where it was deserved, and Leonard had heard a number of nice things said. Rus Emerson had been especially complimentary, and Coach Cade, while less demonstrative than the players, had expressed his approval quite unmistakably. So, all in all, Leonard should have been more than satisfied with the afternoon, it seemed. But he wasn't, for the defeat rankled, and Slim's well-intended but cynical sounding advice to "forget it and wait until next year" brought little comfort. But in spite of having failed in their quest of revenge, the team became quite cheerful, even merry, in fact, before they rolled into Alton, and so Leonard too regained his spirits. It was almost dark by the time he and Slim turned into the yard and made their way toward Haylow, although beyond the buildings the western sky still showed a tint of faded gold most appropriate to the occasion. The Sophomore Dinner was set for seven, and it was already well past five, a fact that Slim mentioned as they reached the front of Academy Hall.

"I ought to get there a bit early, I suppose," he added. "There's usually something that goes wrong at the last minute, and the other fellows on the committee probably won't show up until the last moment."

A dim form detached itself from the shadows of the doorway of Academy once the two had passed and loitered carelessly down the middle path in the direction of the gate. Neither Slim nor Leonard saw this, however. But, just as they went up the steps of Haylow, Leonard laid a detaining hand on his companion's arm.

"There's a fellow behind that tree over there by the yellow house," said Leonard softly. "You can't see him now. He poked his head around just as we started up here."

Slim looked, but the further side of Meadow street was wrapped in shadows and the particular tree, seen between the posts of the entrance, looked no different than other trees. Slim shrugged. "I don't see anything, General. Guess it was just a shadow."

"No, it wasn't. I saw the fellow's head plainly."

"Oh, well, what of it? Probably some kid playing hide-and-seek. I'll tell you, though. We'll have a look from the window at the end of the corridor. Come on."

They climbed the stairs and then went along the second floor hall to the casement that overlooked Meadow street. When they reached it and peered surreptitiously out and down a dark form was proceeding townward along the further sidewalk, beyond the tree. For a brief moment the form was palely lighted as it passed under a street light, and Slim grunted.

"Guess you were right," he said. "Looks like one of the freshies. Keeping tabs on me, I suppose. I wonder if there was anything in Johnny McGrath's guff. Just for fun, when we go in the room we'll have a look before we light up. There may be more of the varmints hiding about."

"What do you suppose they're up to?" asked Leonard.

"Search me," said Slim. Then he chuckled. "Maybe they're going to kidnap us, General. Wish they'd try it, eh?"

"I guess they're not interested in me," replied Leonard a bit regretfully. "See any one?"

He was looking over Slim's shoulder, peering from the darkened window. Outside the Academy yard was black save where the infrequent lights along the walks shed a dim yellow radiance that sent elongated shadows of the nearby trees sprawling off into the gloom. It was a time of evening when most of the fellows were in the dormitories, and save for a boy who passed under the window, whistling a football tune, to turn in at the doorway beneath and come pounding up the stairway, the yard appeared empty. Then Slim said "Humph!" under his breath.

"What?" asked Leonard eagerly.

"Look along the Doctor's path about fifty or sixty feet from the middle path. See anything?"

"N-no," answered Leonard disappointedly.

"Well, I do. There's some one under the tree there. Close up to the trunk and— There! Now he's moving out a bit! See?"

"Yes!" exclaimed the other watcher excitedly. "What do you suppose—"

"Silly chumps," muttered Slim amusedly. "Kid stuff! Oh, well, it amuses them. He'll have to leave there pretty soon and go home to supper, though. That'll be our chance to give them the slip. What time is it, anyhow? Turn on the light, will you?"

"Twenty-two of six," answered Leonard a moment later.

"Plenty of time, then. They can't get out from supper in much less than half an hour, and that'll make it half-past. We'll be gone by—" Slim stopped and listened. "Thought I heard some one outside," he explained, turning his glance away from the closed door. "I was going to say that by half-past six we'll be over at Kingman's. Gee, I'm tired, General! How does my eye look?"

"Not so bad," said Leonard. He felt gingerly of his own nose. "This thing's mighty sore yet. Would you do anything to it?"

"Your beak? No, not until we get back again. Bathe it in arnica then. All it needs now is soap and water."

The youth who had gone pounding up to the floor above a few minutes earlier now came thumping down again. The dormitory was by no means quiet, but the visitor's passing sounded well above all else. Slim frowned. "That's the noisiest brute I ever heard," he muttered. He went over to the window and looked down, but all he could see in the darkness was a dim shape going toward Lykes. "Must be wearing wooden shoes, from the sound." He peered in the direction of the watcher under the tree and then pulled the green shade down. "I hope your feet are cold out there," he muttered.

Both boys laid aside the clothes they had worn to New Falmouth, since, as one never knew just what might occur in the course of a class celebration, it was customary to wear articles that were not highly valued. Slim pulled a pair of gray flannel trousers from the closet and hunted out an old white sweater. Leonard selected a veteran suit of grayish tweed that, during the past summer, had served on Sundays and holidays at the farm. They didn't hurry in their preparations, since, if only as a joke on the freshman spies, they meant to time their trip to the village while the enemy was at supper. Besides, they were both feeling the effects of the game in the shape of lame muscles and a general disinclination to move faster than a slow walk.

Six o'clock struck while they were still dawdling and talking lazily of the afternoon's experiences, and doors began to open along the corridors and the dwellers in Haylow set off for Lawrence Hall and supper. Slim struggled into an old bath-robe and looked around for his slippers. "I sort of think I'll be ready to eat, myself, by the time seven o'clock comes," he remarked. "Where the dickens is that other slipper of mine?"

"I'm ready now," said Leonard. "I hope to goodness nothing happens to that dinner before I get at it!"

"Don't worry, General. Nothing's going to happen to the food. I'll bet that right at this minute Kingman is mounting guard down there with a shot-gun loaded with buckshot!"

"Well, then I hope that nothing happens to keep me from reaching it," amended Leonard, smiling.

Slim chuckled. "That's different," he said. "I'll guarantee the feed, General, but I won't guarantee the guests. Ah, here you are, you lopsided old reprobate!" He pulled the missing slipper from under the further side of his bed and thrust a bare foot into it. "Guess we might as well wash up," he announced. "No use cutting it too fine. I don't run from trouble, but I don't hunt for it, either, and maybe we'll be just as well off if we get inside that restaurant before the freshies finish their supper."

"All right," assented Leonard. The hall was silent now and the last footfall had ceased sounding on the pavement below. He picked up his own robe and threw it over his present scanty costume. At that instant there was an impatient exclamation from Slim.

"What the dickens is the matter with this door?" Slim demanded as he turned the knob and pulled. Then, "Look here, where's the key?" he asked blankly.

The key was always on the inside of the lock, but it plainly wasn't there now. Slim and Leonard both looked about the floor. Then, together, they seized the knob and pulled hard. The door didn't yield.

"Locked!" said Leonard.

Slim nodded, and a broad smile crept over his face. "Locked is right," he chuckled. "The little varmints win the first trick, General!"

"But how? There's been no one here!"

"Remember the fellow with the heavy tread? That's who, I'll bet. Got the tip from the fellow under the tree, or some other fellow, and made a lot of noise going upstairs and then came down again quiet and locked us in."

"But how could he have got the key without our hearing the door open or—" Leonard blinked. "I see! They put the key in the outside before we came home!"

Slim nodded. "Or had it in their pocket. Well, we've got to get out somehow. There's no use raising a riot, for no one will hear us, I guess. Perhaps if we yelled from the window— But, shucks, I wouldn't give those kids the satisfaction! If there was a transom—"

"How about the window?" interrupted Leonard.

"Rather a long drop, General, with a mighty hard landing. Wait a minute! What fellows of our class are in Haylow? Let's see. Joe Conklin's in Number 27, but that's upstairs and on the back. He'd never hear us. He's probably on his way, too. Who else is there?"

"Wharton, in 4," said Leonard. "Let's raise a row and see if anything happens."

They did and nothing did happen. After several minutes of shouting and thumping on the door and banging on the floor with a shoe they gave it up. "Looks now," said Slim, "like I wasn't so smart in deciding to wait! We'd have been wiser if we'd started earlier!" He crossed to the window, threw it wide and looked down. "I guess I can do it," he murmured. Then he glanced to the right and said, "Huh, never thought of that!"

Leonard, a shoe in one hand, was still staring perplexedly at the door when Slim summoned him. "Give me a hand here, General," called Slim. "It's only about five feet to the next window, and I can make it easy."

Slim wriggled out of his robe and kicked off his slippers. Leonard followed him through the window and they stood together on the broad ledge, each with a hand hooked under the sash. "Glad those fresh kids aren't here to see this," commented Slim. "Get hold of my wrist and hold it close in to the wall. If anything happens, son, let go. Don't try to hold me. But I'll make it. All right!"

Slim edged to the end of the ledge, and Leonard slowly followed him. Then, with one hand tight around Slim's right wrist and the other holding fast to the sash, Leonard pressed his body close against the edge of the embrasure while Slim reached out his left hand for a grip on the stone work about the next window. After a moment he said: "Give me another inch or two if you can." Leonard obeyed. There was a moment of suspense and then Slim announced: "All right, General. Let go!" Rather fearfully Leonard released the other's wrist and turned his head to see. Slim was safe on the next sill, raising the lower sash. Then he disappeared, and Leonard climbed back into Number 12. A moment later the door of the next room opened and Slim's bare feet padded along the corridor. A key turned in the lock in front of Leonard and the door swung in.

"Left the key in the lock," panted Slim as he entered. "Say, we'll have to do some hurrying, General! Must be getting close to half-past."

They hustled off to the lavatory and hustled back again and hurriedly donned their clothes. Leonard looked at his watch the instant before he put the light out. The hands pointed to twenty-four minutes after six.

Below, in the half-light of the doorway, Slim paused and looked about inquiringly. There was no one in sight. But as they turned side by side into the middle path that led toward Academy street voices behind them announced that some of the fellows had finished supper and were returning to the dormitories. At the far end of the row, Borden Hall, the freshman dormitory, showed an occasional light, but, so far as either Slim or Leonard could see, no forms were about the entrance. They went on toward the gate, Slim chuckling softly.

"Guess we beat them to it, after all," he said.

But a minute later Slim changed his mind.

CHAPTER XVII
SLIM RETREATS

Just short of the gate the sound of hurrying footsteps brought them sharply around. Behind them, seen dimly, were many approaching forms.

"Let's beat it," whispered Leonard.

"Run from a bunch of freshies?" demanded Slim haughtily. "Not much! We'll turn down Academy street, though, and let them by. If they're up to something we can't stop them here."

Slim led the way sharply to the right, when they were through the gate, and they went on for several rods to pause in the deeper shadow of a not quite leafless tree that overhung the sidewalk. Midway between the infrequent street lights, they were probably invisible to any one at the entrance. A moment or two later a stream of boys appeared. That they were freshmen was conclusively proved by the preponderance of small youths, although quite a good many were fairly big. Some of the throng kept straight ahead across Academy street and disappeared into State street, beyond the corner of the white house where Coach Cade had his lodgings. Others paused before the gate as though for a council, and presently a dozen or more started obliquely across Academy street and went north toward Meadow, half running. Slim and Leonard drew more closely against the fence. The enemy detachment passed on the other side without detecting them and an instant later were visible hurrying around the corner of Meadow street. Meanwhile the rest of the crowd before the gate had, it appeared, reached a decision, for they, too, crossed the road and disappeared into State street, breaking into a run as they passed from sight. Save for an occasional giggle from some over-wrought youngster and a low-toned murmur now and then, the phalanx had come and gone in silence. Leonard thought that silence just a bit depressing!

Left alone on the empty street—empty save for the unseen presence of a lone pedestrian trudging along somewhere in the distance toward River street—Slim whistled softly. "Must have been fully a

124

hundred of them," he marveled. "Now what the dickens are they up to?"

"Looks to me as if they were looking for you," said Leonard.

"Sure, but what can they do if they find me? They don't expect me to stand any of their foolishness, do they? If it came to a scrap—" Slim stopped and looked thoughtfully up and down the dimly lighted street. "Well, let's get along, General. It must be getting close to our dinner time."

"Something tells me," said Leonard sadly, "that I'll never see that dinner!"

Slim chuckled. "Well, to tell the truth, I'm not as sure of it myself as I was! Just the same, General, if those kids are going to keep me away from it they'll have to go some!" He led the way across to the beginning of State street. "Better go this way, I guess," he continued. "They won't be likely to pull any tricks where the bright lights are!"

The bright lights, however, were still a short block away, and when suddenly a gray cat jumped down from a fence-post in front of Leonard and scuttled away almost between his feet that youth gave a yelp of alarm. Slim seemed to consider the incident excruciatingly funny and laughed consumedly. Leonard maintained a haughty silence all the rest of the way to the corner of West street. Here the stores began, and many of them were still open, and their lights combined with the big street lamps made the thoroughfare almost as bright as daylight. No lurking freshman was sighted as the two turned south toward Meadow street, although, since a good many persons were about, scouting members of the enemy forces may have been present. The clock in Tappler's jewelry store proclaimed the time as 6:38 as they passed. As they neared Meadow street Leonard called Slim's attention to two youths who had just come into sight from the direction of the academy. Slim looked and nodded.

"The short fellow's Watkins. I don't know the other one. They're going to the party, I guess."

"Wouldn't it be a good idea to go along with them, Slim? I mean four is better than two if—if there's any trouble."

But Slim shook his head. "No," he answered, "but I tell you what, General. You catch up with them. I'll have a better chance to make it if I'm alone, probably."

"I will not," declared Leonard indignantly. "What do you take me for?"

Slim shrugged. "All right," he said. "I guess there's nothing much up, anyway. We've got lighted streets all the rest of—" He stopped. On the other side of the street as they turned the corner was a group of five older fellows making their way briskly toward the center of town: Red Reilly, Gordon Renneker, Joe Greenwood and two others. "Juniors," said Slim. "Coming to see the fun, I suppose. I'll bet Red's had a lot to do with this business. Don't let them see us, General." Slim slowed his pace a little, and the group across Meadow street passed on, laughing and talking gayly.

"How much further is it?" asked Leonard.

"About five blocks," replied Slim absently. After a moment he said: "Look here, General, I'm wondering if it wouldn't be a clever game to get into Kingman's by the back entrance. It's on Moody street, around the corner from the front door, and I don't believe those fellows know about it."

"Sounds sensible to me," began Leonard.

But Slim disappointed him again. "No, by golly," exclaimed Slim suddenly, "I'm blowed if I'll sneak up any alleys on account of a lot of freshies! We'll go in by the front door, General!"

"Sure," agreed Leonard unenthusiastically. "Just as you say, Slim."

"How are they going to stop us?" Slim went on belligerently. "They can't do it, by gum!"

"Of course not," Leonard assented. "Why, there's only a hundred or so of them. The idea!"

"Well, suppose there are a hundred, or two hundred. They aren't going to—to use their fists, I guess, and if they don't how are they going—"

"I know," said Leonard. "You're probably dead right, Slim, but just the same I'd swap my right to that dinner for a ham sandwich. As the well-known proverb says, Slim, 'A sandwich in the hand is worth two portions of chicken on the plate.'"

"Shut up. Here's High street. The place is in the next block. We'll get there in time, too."

High street proved to be a rather narrow thoroughfare not quite so well lighted as the street they were leaving. The stores had a somewhat second-class appearance and the names on the signs and windows were frequently foreign. In brief, High street impressed one as being a street that had seen better days. The principal shopping thoroughfare lay one block south, and as the boys neared the corner of Moody street the rattle and clang of Market street's traffic was borne to them. And as they neared that corner Leonard exclaimed: "Must be a fire or something, Slim. Look at the crowd!"

A little way beyond the corner of the cross street was a throng that stretched from side to side. Further on, jutting out above the sidewalk on the right, was a gayly illuminated sign that announced in electric lamps: "Kingman's Restaurant." Slim looked and slowed his steps. "Freshies," breathed Slim. "A whole blamed army of 'em, General!"

Leonard could see for himself now that the crowd was composed of boys and knew that Slim was right. The latter drew him aside to the entrance of a shop. "Let's consider a bit," said Slim. "Suppose they've got another gang at the other side, too, eh? Must have, for there's probably not more than fifty in that bunch there." He peered down the street to confirm this statement. Then he laughed. "You're lucky, after all, General," he said. "There's a lunch room right opposite where you can get your sandwich!"

"But what are we going to do?" asked Leonard anxiously.

"Well," answered Slim, "I guess there's just one thing we can do, and that's buck the line. There doesn't seem much chance of running the end, eh? Let's go, General!"

They set forth again side by side, appearing as casual as they might, reached the corner, paused to let an automobile pass and

127

approached the throng. Just then a small youth darted past them and gave the alarm shrilly:

"Staples! Staples!"

A roar of cheers and laughter went up, and the freshman horde moved to meet them. Cries of "Welcome, Soph!" "Dinner's ready, Staples!" "Way for the President!" mingled with jeers and cat-calls.

"Stick behind me," counseled Slim in a low voice. Then he gently pushed the first of the enemy from his path. "Gangway, Fresh," he said smilingly. But they were all about now, presenting a solid barrier. The more Slim shoved the greater the resistance became. He knew better than to lose his patience, however. Instead, he spoke laughingly to Leonard over his shoulder. "Let's go, General," he said. "Play low and make it good!" But although Leonard shoved and pushed there was no advance. "A-a-ay, Soph!" chanted the defenders. Slim felt his dignity slipping fast. He wondered why the fellows upstairs in the restaurant, only a few rods beyond, didn't hear and come to the rescue. But they didn't, and presently, breathless though still smiling, Slim paused to parley.

"What's the big idea, you fellows?" he demanded of one of the bigger freshmen.

"Oh, we like you too well to let you mix in with a lot of low-down trash like those fellows up there," was the flippant reply. "You stay and play with us, Staples."

"Thanks," answered Slim dryly. "All right, but you don't need Grant, too, do you?"

"We-ell," began the boy. But Leonard settled the question himself.

"I'll stay with you, Slim," he announced.

"Say, Staples! Slim Staples, are you hungry?" called some one, and a laugh followed. "Want your dinner, sonny?" "They're just starting on the oysters, Staples!" "Oh, you Sophomore President!"

Stung, Slim faced his tormenters. "What'll you bet I don't get in there?" he demanded warmly.

"When, to-morrow?" asked one of the enemy.

"No, to-night, and before that dinner's over," answered Slim above the burst of laughter that greeted the sally. "You're pretty clever for a bunch of freshies, but then you're *only* freshies, you know!" Slim managed to smile sweetly as he said it, but that didn't make the insult less severe. He took Leonard's arm and turned carelessly away while the crowd jeered more loudly and with the first note of anger. To call a freshman a freshman is, for some reason, the deadliest of insults.

"Sore-head!" some one called shrilly, and "Follow them, Tom!" advised a second. "Better watch 'em!"

Slim turned and leveled a finger at the big leader of the crowd. "Come on," he said. "Follow us. I'd like to have you!"

But the big freshman only grinned and shook his head. "No, thanks," he called after them. "I'll wait here. Come again, Staples, won't you? Dinner's ready!"

Followed by Leonard, Slim walked briskly around the corner of Moody street, but, once out of sight, he slowed down. "Any one after us?" he asked softly.

"No," said Leonard. "Now what, Slim?"

Slim shook his head. "There's the back entrance, but something tells me I didn't do those guys justice. I'm going to have a look, but I don't believe they've left the back door unguarded." He went down the block about half-way and there turned into a narrow alley. Some eighty feet beyond, the forms of a dozen or more youths showed where the dim light from a glass-paneled door fell across the passage. Slim stopped. "You can't fight them," he muttered disgustedly. "They've got us stopped again, General." The two retraced their steps, followed by a jeering shout from the depths of the alley. "We'll go around to Market street," announced Slim, "and think this over. There must be some way!"

CHAPTER XVIII
LEONARD COMES TO THE PARTY

On Market street Slim led the way into a drug store and slipped onto a stool in front of the white marble counter where two aproned youths were dispensing drinks. "We've got to cook up some scheme," he said, "and we might as well be comfortable while we're at it. What's yours?"

"Mine's a good dinner," answered Leonard wistfully.

"You're in the wrong shop, General, but you can have a sandwich if you say the word."

Leonard looked longingly at the two tiers of sandwiches under the glass cover nearby. "You?" he asked.

Slim shook his head sternly. "No, sir, I'm going to dine at Kingman's in about ten minutes."

Leonard sighed and mentioned his choice of a beverage. The renunciation was difficult. When their glasses were in front of them Slim lifted his gravely. "Here's luck," he said.

"Success to our scheme," replied Leonard, and drank deeply. The concoction tasted good and he imbibed again and felt better. He glanced at Slim. Slim was staring hard at the counter and absently tracing a design on its smooth surface. The clock at the end of the store, above the prescription counter, proclaimed three minutes past seven. Leonard looked out through the big glass window and sought inspiration. The sidewalks were well thronged, for the evening was mild for November. A big yellow trolley car passed with a strident clanging of its gong. Automobiles went by honking warningly to the rash pedestrians who sought to find their way across the street. A smart looking policeman, his fingers crooked in his belt, paused momentarily to view the contents of the window and then continued on his beat. Leonard had found his inspiration.

"Slim, look here," he exclaimed. "Why can't we get a cop to put us through that mob back there? I just saw one go by. If we told him how it was—"

But Slim looked instantly disapproving. "That wouldn't be playing the game," he answered. "You—you don't call on the cops to help you, General. It isn't done."

"That wouldn't be playing the game," he answered

"Isn't done be blowed!" said Leonard. "Look here, I'm so hungry I could eat nails. We didn't have enough lunch to keep a canary alive, Slim. I want my dinner, and if I can get it by hooking onto a cop—"

"You'd bring disgrace on the whole Sophomore Class," interrupted the other. "No, not to be thought of, General. Besides, I've got a better plan."

"It's about time," grumbled Leonard.

"What's to keep us from getting a taxi and going right to the door of the restaurant?"

"Why, you poor boob, those wild Indians would halt the taxi and see you inside. They'll be looking for some such scheme as that."

"I guess you're right," acknowledged Slim sadly. "You're next."

"Well, suppose we got the restaurant on the telephone and told the bunch that we were on the corner and couldn't get by. Then they could come out and rescue us."

"Ye-es, but that would be sort of babyish, wouldn't it? I'd a heap rather get there by my own—er—efforts."

"So would I," responded Leonard a trifle impatiently, "but your own efforts aren't getting us there! And—and it's getting late!"

The clock said eight minutes past now. The two subsided into silence again. Slim set down his empty glass. "Want another?" he asked morosely. Leonard shook his head. Half a hundred more precious seconds passed and then Leonard gave an exclamation of triumph. "Got it!" he declared. "Got it, Slim! At least, I think so. How does this strike you?"

Pushing aside his glass, Leonard bent his head close and explained his project, while Slim, at first looking dubious, at last nodded in wholehearted approval. "Sure!" he said with conviction. "That'll do it, I'll bet, General. But, hold on, how about you? That sort of leaves you out in the storm, doesn't it?"

"Never mind me," said Leonard. "You're the important one. Besides, I'll make it somehow later. All I ask you to do is to see that there's something left when I do get there."

"Well," said Slim, "if you don't get in when I do I'll take a bunch and go out and get you."

"Thought you said that sort of thing was babyish? No, you just see that there's something left, Slim, and leave the rest to me. I guess they won't care whether I make it or not. It's only you, as the Class President, who interests them."

Slim looked doubtful, but time was passing and he had thrown down the gauntlet to the Freshman Class. "All right," he agreed. "Have it your way. Let's go."

"Wait a minute," objected Leonard. "We've got it wrong. We'd both better try the same end of the block. They've seen you in that white sweater there and won't be looking for you in anything else. See what I mean?"

"Yes, and I guess you're right, General. And say, old son, as a general you're sure making good!"

About five minutes later the watchful-waiting throng of freshmen at the Moody street end of the block again rushed into barricade formation, spurred on by the joyous applause of a score of juniors who, having stationed themselves inside the barricade in the hope of witnessing some fun, were finding the proceedings rather tame. A rickety taxi had swung around from Market street and was attempting to penetrate the barrier. The freshmen rallied to the threatened invasion.

"Stop that taxi!" was the slogan. "Look inside!"

Opposed by a solid mass of humanity, there was nothing for the driver of the vehicle to do but stop. He did so, protesting forcibly and most impolitely. The freshmen swarmed about the dilapidated taxicab, breasting the sizzling radiator and showering questions on the fuming proprietor. Others peered in through the glass. Suspense and confusion reigned. On the corner a policeman twirled his club and looked on in good-natured amusement. On such occasions as this the Law was ever lenient with youth. The suspense was short-lived. A cry of joyous triumph arose and the doors of the cab were snatched open.

"Here he is!" was the cry. "Trying to sneak past! Nothing doing, Staples! Try again, Soph!"

"Pull him out!" advised a fellow well removed from the center of the crowd.

"Turn around, cabby! No thoroughfare, old sport! Detour by Market street. Police orders."

Then of a sudden triumph came to an end. A disgusted voice arose above the joyous clamor. "It isn't Staples! It's only General Grant!"

"What!" "You're crazy!" "Let's see!" "Show us!" "Oh, shucks!"

Leonard was extremely dignified throughout what was, quite naturally, an annoying experience to a peaceful traveler of the city streets. "You fellows haven't any right," he said firmly, "to stop this taxi. I've paid the driver to take me to Kingman's Restaurant, and—"

"Sorry, Grant, but this street's barred to traffic." The snub-nosed freshman blocking the door on one side grinned exasperatingly. Behind him, his companions pushed and shoved in an effort to see into the dark interior of the cab.

"Look on the floor, Higbee! Bet you Staples is in there!" some one shouted. Hands explored the corners and one boy produced a flash light and cast its rays about. Disappointment was writ large on the countenances of all. "Not here!" was proclaimed.

"Where'd he go?" asked Higbee, who appeared to be one of the leading spirits.

"Who?" asked Leonard densely.

"Slim Staples. Where'd he get to?"

"Oh, Slim?" Leonard leaned out of one door and looked up the block. In front of the well-lighted and for the moment unguarded entrance to the restaurant, a tall youth paused to wave a hand ere he disappeared. Leonard laughed softly. "Why," he went on, "Slim's just gone in to dinner."

"Yes, he has!" jeered Higbee. But others had seen the incident, although too late to interfere, and the dire news was being shouted up and down the block.

"He got in! I saw him!" "Oh, your grandmother! How could he?" "Yes, he did! Arthur saw him, too! He stopped at the door and waved—" "What's that? Staples made it? When? How could he? What? Walked right in the door! Say, where were you guys? You were supposed to—" "Come on! Let's stop him! Where'd he go? Who saw him?" "They say he got in!" "Rot! He's in the crowd somewhere! This cab was a stall! Come on, Freshmen!"

Such a hullabaloo! Leonard, laughing, awaited his chance. It came. The defenders of the Moody street approach forgot him entirely and went rushing toward the door of the restaurant. Leonard slipped swiftly from the cab and followed, taking his place in the rear ranks of the enemy. The driver of the taxi, his fifty cents safely in his pocket, chuckled and swung back toward Market street.

Something over a hundred freshmen came together in a confused, pushing, shoving mass before the restaurant entrance. Accusations of dereliction of duty were frequent. Denials answered them. The masterful Higbee, striving to make his voice heard above the tumult, demanded proof. Assertions and denials battled for supremacy. Staples had gone in. Staples hadn't gone in. Lots of fellows had seen him. They were crazy. Higbee waved a hand in exasperation. The policeman from the corner appeared suddenly in the scene, his good-natured voice mildly exhorting them to "move on now and don't be blocking the sidewalk." Slowly they gave back, flocking into the street. Across the thoroughfare the group of juniors, laughing enjoyably, forgot their neutral status and proffered wicked advice.

"Go on up and get him, Freshies! Don't let him fool you that way!"

Fortunately perhaps, the noise was still too great for the advice to reach the freshmen. And just then a window went up on the second floor of the building, and the shade was pushed aside. *"Oh, Fresh!"* Comparative silence fell, and the crowd in the street craned their heads and sought the voice, slowly backing from the entrance in their effort to see. *"Oh, Fresh!"* Again the mocking challenge. A mutter arose from the throng that grew rapidly into a roar of futile rage. At the window Slim Staples smiled benignly down and waved a gay hand.

"Who wins the bet?" he called.

"A cold dinner for you, Slim!" shouted a freshman shrilly. A shout of approval went up, but Slim shook his head.

"Haven't started yet," he answered. "Oysters just coming up!" Grinning faces appeared behind Slim's at the window. "Now then, fellows, three hearty groans for the Freshman Class!"

With a final wave of his hand, Slim disappeared, the window closed, and the long white shade fell back into place. A dismal silence held the throng below. Only the unkind laughter of the juniors disturbed the quiet of the moment. And in that moment, made desperate by Slim's mention of oysters, a boy in a white sweater that was somewhat too large for him, detached himself swiftly from the group and sped toward the doorway. The shout of warning came too late. So, too, did the effort of the startled policeman. The latter's hands came away empty, and Leonard, caroming from a corner of the doorway, righted himself and went scurrying up the flight of stairs.

At the top he paused for an instant to glance behind. The policeman was trying to do two things at once and succeeding. He was peering undecidedly after the trespasser and holding back the pursuit. With an unsteady laugh Leonard tried the knob of the door in front of him, from behind which came the sounds of a merry party. It did not yield. Leonard tried again and put his weight against the portal. From below came the hoarse voice of the officer.

"Hey, youse, come down out of that before I comes up and gets you!"

Leonard beat a tattoo on the door. The policeman started slowly and heavily and remorselessly up the carpeted steps. Behind him the doorway was crowded with faces. Leonard kicked until the door shook.

"Let me in, Sophs! This is Grant!" he shouted.

"Come away from that now!" ordered the policeman gruffly. He was almost at the top, and Leonard's brief glance told him that his good-nature was no longer to be relied on.

"I've got a right in here," panted Leonard, still pounding and kicking. "I'm—I'm one of the party!"

"Your party's down below," answered the officer grimly, and, topping the last step, stretched out a massive hand. Leonard, backed against the door now, waved weakly at the menace and tried to find words. Then, just when the Law was about to clutch him, the door behind him opened suddenly and unexpectedly and Leonard arrived on the scene of the Sophomore Dinner in most undignified manner!

The door closed as quickly as it had opened, leaving a surprised policeman to scratch his head and, finally, to retrace his steps to the sidewalk, where his appearance empty-handed summoned a groan of disappointment from the waiting throng. That disappointment was the last straw, and, after a rather half-hearted cheer for themselves, the freshmen wended their way back to school.

Upstairs, Leonard was finishing his sixth and final oyster.

CHAPTER XIX
NOT ELIGIBLE

After a day like yesterday only one thing could be expected of the weather, and so here was a rainy Sunday. After church came dinner, and after dinner—well, nothing, it seemed, but a long and sleepy afternoon. Leonard and Slim found reading matter and settled down, Slim on the window-seat because he managed to reach it first, and Leonard on his bed, with his own and Slim's pillows under his head. Outside the November afternoon was dark with lead-gray clouds and a fine, persistent rain challenged Leonard's optimistic prediction of clearing weather by four o'clock. Slim grunted gloomily and hunched himself more comfortably against the cushions. "It's days like this," he said, "that account for the startling prevalence of crime during the month of November in American preparatory schools."

At three Leonard laid down his book, yawned and looked through the window. It wasn't raining as it had been an hour ago; it was raining harder! "As a weather prophet," reflected Leonard, "I'm a flivver." He yawned again. Then: "Let's put on our coats, Slim, and get out," he suggested. "This is deadly." There was, however, no response, and Leonard lifted himself on an elbow and looked across. Slim's book was laid flat across his chest, and he was fast asleep. "Sluggard!" grumbled Leonard. He pillowed his head in his hands and considered. He might go to sleep, too, but he didn't want to. He might arouse Slim and persuade him to go out. Or he might let poor old Slim alone and splash over to The Hill and see Johnny McGrath. That's what he would do!

His final act before leaving the room was to slip a piece of paper between Slim's gently folded hands. On the paper was written: "Gone to Europe. Back at five. Sweet dreams." Mrs. McGrath answered Leonard's ring and told him that Johnny was up in his room and that he should go right up. Meanwhile she divested Leonard of his dripping mackinaw and bore it off to the nearest radiator to dry. Johnny was hunched in a big chair when Leonard reached the head of the stairway and could see into the room. His knees were close to his chin, and a big book was propped against them. But the book was quickly laid aside when he saw the visitor. He pushed a chair close to the radiator and forced Leonard into it, bidding him put his feet to the warmth, and then drew up a second chair for himself, beaming welcome the while.

"Sure, you're an angel," he declared, "to drop in like this, General. Where's Slim that he isn't with you?"

"Fast asleep, the lazy coot. I guess last evening was too much for him, Johnny." They had progressed to the stage where "McGrath" had given place to "Johnny." "Did you hear about it?"

Johnny nodded and laughed. "Yes, young Shawley was telling me this morning. I'm sorry I didn't go down and see the fun. You and Slim were too smart for them, eh?"

"Well, we got there, although I'll confess they had us worried for awhile. What I don't understand is why they locked us in the room. They must have known we'd have got out sooner or later."

Johnny nodded again. "I'll tell you about that. 'Twas Reilly put the freshmen up to it, or most of it. They had it planned, they thought, so Slim couldn't get to the dinner. They expected he'd start early, and there was about twenty of the freshies waiting for him down by the gate, where they could have got him either way he'd gone."

"Got him?" queried Leonard.

"Oh, sure, nothing rough, you understand. But they had a fake note from Coach Cade asking Slim to stop and see him, and one of them was to give it to him, the rest being out of sight. The coach went away over Sunday at five-forty, but Reilly had in some way got him to leave the key to his rooms. Well, the plan was that Slim was to call at the house over there on the corner, and some one was to say 'Come in,' and the room would be dark and then, the first thing Slim would know he'd be safe in the big closet for the evening."

"But Slim knew—we both knew—that Mr. Cade was going home, Johnny."

"Maybe, but likely he wouldn't have remembered it, or perhaps he'd have figured that Mr. Cade was going on a later train. Anyway, that's how they had it fixed. But you fellows didn't start along early enough, and the gang had to go to supper. So Shawley locked you in the room, to keep you there until they could get out from supper. He'd swiped the key earlier in the afternoon, do you see. Well, when you did start out they knew it was too late to spring that fake note on you and so they fixed to keep you away from the restaurant. That is, Slim. They didn't care so much whether you got there. You were only a—a complication, as you might say. Remember, I tipped Slim off the other evening. I didn't know then what the scheme was, but I knew they were after him."

"So that was it," mused Leonard. "We saw the freshies hiding around behind trees when we got back from the game, but I didn't suppose they meant anything much. Neither did Slim; until we found ourselves locked in the room."

"How was it Slim got there finally?" asked Johnny. "Young Shawley says you were in a taxicab, with Slim's white sweater on—"

"Yes, we changed clothes. That is, I put on Slim's sweater and he put on my coat and an old felt hat I was wearing. You see, they'd already seen Slim with that sweater on, and so they'd be looking for it again. I got in the taxi on Market street and Slim walked away around by Morrison street, coming back on Moody. We'd fixed 'zero hour' at seven fifteen so he'd have time to get to the corner when I did. Of course the freshies thought I was Slim as soon as they saw the white sweater, and I didn't show myself before I had to. Slim just walked into the crowd, with my hat pulled down over his face, and while the freshies were all clustered around the taxi he sauntered along down the street, no one paying any attention to him. It was as easy as pie."

"Sure, I wish I'd been there," chuckled Johnny. "And they say you butted a cop out of your way afterwards and no one could stop you!"

"I didn't butt him. He made a dive at me and I side-stepped, showing the value of football training, Johnny."

"Did you have a good dinner?"

"Did we? Wow! And, gee, I was so hungry I couldn't eat fast enough. We didn't get through until half-past nine, pretty nearly!"

"I suppose you heard about Renneker and Jimsy Carnochan?" asked Johnny.

"No. Who's Jimsy— Oh, I remember! What's happened?"

"Sure, nothing much—yet," answered Johnny, "but I'm fearing something may. It seems that Jimsy and a couple of other town fellows were coming along River street last night when Renneker and Red Reilly and three or four other chaps were coming back to school. They'd been over watching the freshies, you know."

"I know; we passed them," assented Leonard.

"Well, I got it from Jimsy this forenoon after church. According to his tell, our gang was taking up the whole sidewalk, walking five or six abreast, maybe, and one of the fellows with Jimsy objected and shoved into them, and there were some words. Jimsy says the juniors started the trouble, but maybe he's prejudiced. Anyhow, he and Renneker squared off and punched each other a couple of times, no harm being done, do you see, and the others shoving in spoiling it. From what Jimsy says, I get it that Renneker laughed and wanted to shake hands, and Jimsy was still ugly. He's that way when he's mad. He said something to Renneker about 'having the goods on him,' and then Renneker and the others went on. Well, now Jimsy's awfully sore, General, and I'm fearful he'll be telling what he knows around town, and it'll get to the Academy. I argued with him, but he's stubborn. There's English blood in him, I'm thinking."

Leonard laughed. "That's what makes him stubborn, eh?"

Johnny grinned. "Sure it is," he answered stoutly. "Every one knows the English are mules for stubbornness."

"Oh, well, he'll probably get over his grouch," said Leonard cheerfully. "And, even if he should spill the beans, it wouldn't be likely to reach faculty's ears."

"Maybe not," allowed Johnny. "Not that I'd trouble much if it did, for it looks to me like this big fellow isn't any marvel, anyway, and some one else might play his position fully as well and maybe better." He looked meaningly at Leonard, but the latter chose to disregard the insinuation.

"Gordon Renneker's playing a lot better game than he did awhile back, Johnny. Yesterday he was corking in the last part of the game with New Falmouth."

"It might be," Johnny admitted. "I didn't go. But if I was you I'd be sort of glad if Renneker wasn't around, General."

"Oh, nonsense! There's still Stimson and Raleigh and Falls."

"You've got Raleigh and Falls beat right now," declared the other with deep conviction. "And I wouldn't wonder if you could play as good a game as either of the others, in spite you aren't so big."

"You're crazy," laughed Leonard. "Anyway, Johnny, I'm not kicking. I do think that Mr. Cade will give me a show in the Oak Grove game next Saturday, and if I make good in that it's likely I'll get into the Kenly Hall fracas for a time."

"This Oak Grove game's the last before the big one, isn't it?" mused Johnny. Leonard nodded. "Then you've got only the two weeks," continued the other reflectively. "Man, you've got to work! My money's on you, though, General, and whether this big fellow is playing or isn't playing I'll be looking for you to be right there when the last fight starts."

"I wish I had your confidence, Johnny," laughed Leonard. "Unless by 'right there' you mean on the bench."

"I do not," said Johnny decisively. "I mean playing at right guard or left and giving the other fellows what-for!"

"Oh, well, I hope you're right."

"I know I'm right."

"Any English blood in you?" asked Leonard.

Yet on Monday it almost seemed that Johnny's hopefulness was not without cause, for Leonard found himself treated with a new—well, deference is hardly the word: let us say respect, although even that word is scarcely the right one. Call it what you like, however, and the fact remains that the new order of things entailed much harder work than Leonard had done before. With less than two weeks remaining before the final contest of the season, Coach Cade appeared to be striving to present a team of worn-out and exhausted cripples for Kenly Hall's amusement. Yet, probably because he had brought them along fairly slowly so far, the players proved capable of performing a lot of work and receiving a lot of punishment in that fortnight. The time had come to round off the corners, to smooth down the rough places, to acquire subtleties without forgetting fundamentals. There were new plays to learn, too, and, a little later, new signals. Perhaps Leonard worked no harder than any one else; perhaps, because he had more to learn, it just seemed harder. But he got on famously. There was no doubt about that. He was fast and mettlesome and used his head. By the last of the week he had been accepted by those in the know—and some who weren't—as a certain performer against Kenly Hall. When he spoke of sore muscles or contused shins or strained ligaments Slim browbeat him shamefully.

"What of it?" Slim would demand fiercely. "Expect to play football without getting bruised a little? Don't be a pill. Why, you've got Renneker and Stimson lying awake nights trying to think up some way of beating you! Here, let's see your old leg. Where's that bottle of arnica? Hold still, you silly ass! Sure, I knows it hurts, but you needn't throw a fit about it!"

"Fit yourself!" Leonard would snap indignantly, being thoroughly weary and sore all over. "Look at the way you went on when you got a black eye that time!"

"It wasn't the bruise I minded, it was simply the damage to my manly beauty. These sore places of yours won't ever show, General, even if you play in a bathing-suit!"

Then, on Friday, Jimsy Carnochan returned from a brief visit to New London and took his pen in hand, thereby considerably "gumming up" the Alton Academy football situation.

To Jimsy's credit be it said that he didn't hide behind any such anonymity as "A Friend" or "Wellwisher" or "Fair Play." No, sir, Jimsy came right out and signed the bottom of that chirographic bombshell plainly with his name, thus: "James Duffy Carnochan." It was a bombshell, too, if for no other reason than that it exploded so unexpectedly. It was addressed to Coach Cade, and it reached that already harassed gentleman by the first mail delivery on Saturday morning. It ran as follows:

> Mr. John Cade,
> 87 Academy street,
> City.

DEAR SIR:

You might like to know that one of your football players isn't eligible to play on your team. His name is Renneker but it wasn't that last August when he played first baseman for the Maple Leafs baseball team of New London, it was George Ralston. He got twenty-five dollars for playing first baseman and if you don't believe it please communicate with John Worrall in Care Broady Silk Mill, New London. Worrall managed the Maple Leafs and paid the money to Ralston or Renneker cash before the game started, as he will tell you. I guess he can't deny it anyway, not if you ask him right out.

Wishing you a successful season,

> Resply yours,
> JAMES DUFFY CARNOCHAN.

Coach Cade frowned, read the epistle a second time, laughed shortly and thrust it into a pocket. He had received similar communications before to-day, sometimes written in good faith, sometimes purely mischievous. Then he reflected that here must be an example of the former sort, since the writer had not only signed his name but, evidently as an after-thought, placed an address on the flap of the envelope. Nevertheless, in the press of other matters Coach Cade forgot the letter for several hours, and it wasn't until he pulled it forth from his pocket when seeking another document that he recalled its annoying existence. This was just after early dinner was over at training table, and Gordon Renneker was still in sight by the dining hall door. The coach excused himself to Tod Tenney and made after the player.

"Renneker," he said, overtaking the big fellow just outside the hall, "got a minute to spare?"

Renneker assented and followed the other along the path that led around to the gymnasium. Coach Cade produced the letter and handed it to Renneker. "Got that in the morning's mail," he explained. "I'm not taking any stock in it, you understand, but you'd better see it."

Gordon Renneker read the epistle through calmly and handed it back, with a smile. The smile, however, was not quite natural, and the coach noted the fact. "Well," he asked, "what about it?"

"I'd say," replied Renneker, "it's a case of mistaken identity."

"Probably," agreed Johnny, eyeing him sharply nevertheless. "I presume you never played baseball on this team?"

"No," answered the other. The coach waited for further words, but Renneker seemed to have finished with the subject. The coach frowned. He put the letter back into a pocket.

"Know this fellow Carnochan?" he asked.

"No. I never heard of him before."

"H'm, funny he has it in for you, then."

Renneker shrugged. "He may know me, Coach," he suggested. "I think I'll look the beggar up and ask him what's on his mind. What's the address? Mind if I have the letter?"

"I'll give you the address and you can set it down. Got a pencil? '164 Orchard street, 2nd Bell.' You know, of course, that if you had played on that team, and received money for doing it, you couldn't play here, Renneker."

"Naturally."

"All right. When you see this chap you'd better convince him that he's mistaken. We don't want him writing that sort of a letter to Kenly Hall or shooting off his mouth to the newspapers."

"He wouldn't do that, would he?" exclaimed Renneker with evident dismay. "Talk to the newspapers, I mean."

"I don't know, son. Look here, Renneker, there's something in this. You'd better come clean, my boy, and save trouble later."

There was no answer for a minute. Renneker was studying the ground intently. Coach Cade didn't like the look on his face. Finally Renneker looked up and laughed shortly.

"I fancy you're right," he said. "I'll hand in my togs."

"What! But, great Scott, man, you don't mean to tell me—"

"I'm not telling anything," answered Renneker evenly. "I'm just not denying."

"And you came here with this thing hanging over your head and let us waste our time on you, knowing that it was bound to come out! Renneker, I'd like to—to—"

"Wrong, sir. I didn't know it would come out. I'm sorry. If there's anything more I can say, I'll say it, but it doesn't occur to me at the moment. I'm just—awfully sorry, Mr. Cade."

He turned and went off, unhurriedly, shoulders back.

CHAPTER XX
RIGHT GUARD GRANT

Captain Emerson, Billy Wells, Bee Appel and Perry Stimson had gone over to Lakeville to watch Kenly Hall play Rutledge. Consequently Alton faced Oak Grove that afternoon minus the services of five of her best players. Kerrison took Rus's place at right end, Wilde substituted for the "demon tackle," as Slim called Billy Wells, Carpenter went in at quarter, a newcomer named Grant played right guard and Raleigh played left. Probably Coach Cade could have sprinkled in half a dozen third-string players beside and still seen the contest won by the Gray-and-Gold, for Oak Grove, selected for the last game but one because she was never formidable, proved weak beyond expectation. Alton piled up three scores in the first two periods, for a total of 21 points, and held the visitor to a field-goal. When the third quarter started Cruikshank was at the helm, and Goodwin, Kendall and Dakin completed the backfield. As the final half progressed other substitutions took place and when the last whistle blew only one man was on who had started the contest, and that man was Sam Butler. Leonard stayed on until the fourth period and then gave way to Falls. Two more scores, a touchdown and a field-goal by Kendall from the thirty-four yards, had added 10 points more to an impressive total. Oak Grove had, however, in the third period taken advantage of a fumble by Cruikshank and banged her way through for a touchdown, and the final figures were 31 to 10.

Leonard played a good if not startling game at right guard that afternoon. Perhaps he would have performed better had there been more incentive, but Oak Grove's inferiority had shown early in the game, and Alton's first two scores had been made before the first period was done, and one doesn't fight as hard against a vanquished opponent as against one who still threatens. Besides that, Leonard's adversaries—there were two of them—were not difficult. On the whole, that game proved scarcely good practice for the home team.

What had happened to Gordon Renneker was a question that many asked, for the former right guard was neither on the side-line or in the stand. Some insisted that he had accompanied the scouts to

Lakeville, but that explanation was refused by others who had seen him at least an hour after dinner time. Leonard wondered and speculated, too, but it wasn't until Johnny McGrath dropped in at Number 12 Haylow that evening, just as Slim and Leonard were starting for the movies, that the matter was cleared up for him. Jimsy Carnochan, it seemed, had met Johnny on the street just before supper and confessed to having written to Coach Cade.

"I guess he was sort of sorry he'd done it," said Johnny, "but he wouldn't say so. Maybe I didn't read the riot-act to him, though! We nearly had a scrap!"

"I hope he chokes!" commented Slim bitterly. "That was a swell thing to do, just before the Kenly game! Leaves us flat for a right guard, and no time to find one. He ought to be—be—"

"I guess it was more my fault than any one's," said Johnny regretfully. "I shouldn't have lugged him to the game that time and let him see Renneker."

"You bet you shouldn't," agreed Slim heartily. But Leonard demurred.

"Piffle," he said, "Johnny isn't to blame. Better blame Renneker for getting fresh the other night and getting Carnochan down on him. Maybe we're taking too much for granted, anyway, fellows. Maybe Mr. Cade just kept Renneker out of to-day's game while he looks into the business."

"Renneker wasn't at training table for supper," said Slim. "That means that he's done for. I call it a pretty rotten piece of business!"

They lugged Johnny along to the pictures and discussed the matter very thoroughly both going and returning. Slim agreed eventually that maybe Leonard would hold down Renneker's position satisfactorily, but they couldn't get him to acknowledge that Mr. Cade had acted rightly in dismissing Renneker from the team. He said some very disapproving things of the coach, sneered at him for being a "Lily-white" and doubted that he or any one else could present adequate proof that Renneker had received money for playing baseball. Especially, however, he was bitter against Carnochan, and would have sought that gentleman out and presented him with a piece of his mind had not Leonard and Johnny dissuaded him. In the end they all agreed that it was up to them to keep what they knew to themselves, and by Monday they were very glad that they had, for Gordon Renneker was out on the field in togs coaching the guards and the news was abroad that he had been dropped because of difficulties with the Office. That was such a plausible explanation that no one doubted it, although one might have wondered how it was that he was allowed to aid in the coaching. The incident seemed to have made no great difference to Renneker. He was perhaps a bit more stand-offish than ever and inclined to sarcastic criticisms that seldom failed to get under the skin of Raleigh, who, worried over his failure to make progress that fall, was in no mood for the big fellow's caustic humor. That the two never quite came to blows was chiefly due to the fact that practice came to an end just before Raleigh's patience did.

Leonard had definitely taken Renneker's position. Had Leonard had any doubt about it Coach Cade's announcement on Tuesday would have dispelled it. "You'll start the Kenly game, Grant," said the coach after practice that afternoon, "and I expect you to show me that I haven't made a mistake in selecting you instead of Falls. You've done very well indeed so far. You play a fast, heady game, my boy, and I'll say frankly that when you've two or three more inches and another twenty pounds on you you'll be a mighty good guard. You've got faults, but I hope you'll get rid of most of them by Saturday. Starting before the ball is one of them. Tenney has four cases marked against you, and just because you've got by so far without being penalized doesn't mean that you won't get caught finally. And when an official once finds a player off-side he watches that player hard ever after; and sometimes he sees faults where there aren't any, without meaning to. It's just a case of giving a dog a bad name. I want you to steady down and look out for that trouble. Another thing, Grant, is over-eagerness to get through. It's a good fault, if any fault can be said to be good, but it works against the play sometimes. Frequently you're across the line when you ought to be still on your own side, which means that you're out of the play when you might be helping it along. When you get your signal think what it means. Think where the play's going and what your part is in it. Don't break through and think afterwards, Grant.

You've got a good nose for the ball, but don't let it run away with you. It's a fine thing to be able to put your man out and then get down the field under a punt, but we've got ends and backs to do that trick. Your part is to guard your center until the ball is passed, on attack, and then make the hole or stop the other fellow from coming through. In other words, you're a bulldog first and a grayhound afterwards. Once you've done your duty thoroughly I don't care how hard you go after the ball, but don't skimp the duty. Sure first and then fast, ought to be your motto, my boy. How are you feeling?"

"Fine," answered Leonard stoutly.

The coach smiled. "Good! What's the matter with that ankle?"

"Ankle?" repeated Leonard innocently.

"Yes, the left one. You've been limping, you know."

"Oh, that! Why, nothing at all, sir. I gave it a sort of a turn, you know."

"Tell the trainer to look at it, and don't forget it."

Captain Emerson and his brother scouts had brought back scant information from the Kenly Hall-Rutledge game. Rutledge had been outclassed from the first, and, without showing too much of her possibilities, Kenly had piled up 16 points against her while keeping her own goal intact. Kenly had made an average showing during the season. She had played one more game than Alton and had won all but two of them. Lorimer had beaten her decisively and Middleboro had tied her at 7 to 7. She had, for her, a light team, but one that was capable of speed and versatility. She had specialized in forward-passing during the early part of the season, but of late had fallen back on line plays for her gains, although signs were not wanting that forward-passes were still in her repertory. Briefly, Kenly Hall School was rather more of a mystery to her ancient rival this year than she generally was, and, since it is human nature to fear the unknown, there was less confidence at Alton than was usual before the big game.

The eleventh-hour loss of Gordon Renneker was a severe blow to most followers of the game at Alton. There were many who believed, not a few very ardently, in Leonard Grant's ability to completely fill Renneker's shoes, but they were in the minority. It stood to reason, naturally, that a youngster like Grant, lacking size, weight and experience could not wholly take the place of an All-Scholastic star. Leonard himself agreed with the majority. Oddly enough, Gordon Renneker did not. This was divulged on Wednesday when, after a half-hour of strenuous work for the guards and tackles and centers, the little squad returned to the bench and blankets to await their call to the scrimmage. Leonard found Renneker beside him when he had pulled the gray blanket around him. So far what might be called personal intercourse between them had been limited to those few words exchanged in the taxicab on the occasion of their arrival at Alton two months before. Now, after a moment, Renneker said abruptly:

"You're going mighty well, Grant."

"Thanks," Leonard stammered. In spite of himself, he still found it impossible not to be impressed and a bit awed by Renneker's imperturbable air of superiority.

"I don't see why you shouldn't hold down that place as well as I could have done," the other continued thoughtfully. "Hope so. Nasty trick, my getting dropped, Grant. I wouldn't want the team to suffer by it. I don't fancy it will, though, if you play the way I think you can."

"Well, I don't know," muttered the other. "Aren't you—isn't there any chance of you getting in Saturday?"

"Oh, dear, no," replied Renneker calmly. "Not a chance."

"I'm sorry," said Leonard. Renneker turned a slow glance on him. Then: "Thanks, but it's of no consequence," he said.

He nodded carelessly, arose and sauntered away.

Leonard wondered why he had asked such an idle question. He had known well enough that Renneker wouldn't get back. He felt very sorry for him just then.

Later, he told Slim what Renneker had said, and Slim frowned and grunted: "Mighty decent of him, I'll say."

Leonard assented, but with too little enthusiasm to satisfy the other. "If it was me," Slim went on, "I guess I wouldn't be talking like that to you. I'd be feeling too sore about losing my position."

"Well, but it isn't my fault he's off the team," objected Leonard, mildly.

Slim grunted again. "Never mind; he's off, and that's what counts!"

Leonard felt that there was something wrong somewhere in Slim's point of view, but he was too tired to pursue the matter.

There was a short session against the second team on Thursday, and then the whistle blew for the last time, and the season on Alton Field was at an end. The second cheered and was cheered and, finally, followed by the onlookers, crossed back to their own field and started a fire. A battered and discarded football, bearing a leering countenance painted on with white pigment, was set atop the pyre and the scrubs joined hands and danced riotously around it. The fact that the football subsided into ruins with only a faint sigh, instead of expiring with a resonant *bang*, was accepted as an ill omen of Saturday's game. But the omen did not appear to affect the second team spirits appreciably!

Friday was a day of rest, but there was an hour of signal drill in the gymnasium in the afternoon and a brief blackboard lecture by the coach in the evening. The latter was over by eight-fifteen, however, and afterwards Slim tried to persuade Leonard to accompany him to the final mass meeting in the auditorium. But Leonard had no mind for it, and Slim, realizing that his friend was having a mild attack of nerves, didn't persist long. Going out, he stopped at the door to say: "I wouldn't think too much about to-morrow, General; about the game, you know. Better get a good story and read. I'll be back soon."

Leonard was willing to follow the other's advice, but it wasn't so easy. And when he looked for the good story it wasn't to be found. At length he decided to walk over to the library and get a book, although, since the auditorium was above the library, he had no intention of tarrying there. It was a nice night, just frostily cold and with a couple of trillions of white stars winking away in a blue-black sky. Even with his mackinaw unbuttoned he was quite comfortable. Long before he neared Memorial he could hear the singing.

"Cheer for the Gray-and-Gold!
Flag of the brave and bold—"

A long, measured cheer followed the last strain, and then came silence. No, not silence, for Leonard was close to the building now and could hear at intervals a word or two. Some one was speaking. There was a sudden burst of applause, quickly suppressed. Then he was entering the library. The long room with its mellow warmth and its two rows of cone-shaped green shades was deserted save for the presence in a corner of a small freshman hunched absorbedly over a book. Leonard paused outside the door, suddenly distasteful of libraries and books. Then he turned back and went down the steps again. It was far nicer outdoors, he thought. He would cross the grass to River street and walk around by Academy and Meadow to the farther gate. Probably by the time he reached the room again Slim would have returned, and then he could go to bed. Not, however, that bed held any great appeal, for he was quite sure he wouldn't be able to get to sleep for hours.

Short of the first street light, that on the corner, he descried a shape ahead of him. Some one else, it appeared, scorned indoors to-night. The shape was tall and broad, and Leonard suspected one of the faculty, perhaps Mr. Screven, and hoped that he could get by without having to say more than "Good evening." He couldn't imagine anything more deadly than being obliged to loll along and listen to Mr. Screven's monotonous voice. But, a few paces behind now, he saw that the solitary pedestrian was not Mr. Screven, was not, indeed, a faculty at all, but Gordon Renneker.

CHAPTER XXI
RENNEKER EXPLAINS

Leonard was still assimilating that fact when Renneker turned and recognized him in the light of the corner lamp. "Hello, Grant," said the big fellow. There seemed to Leonard a tone of almost friendliness in that greeting.

"Hello," he answered. He wanted to add something else, something about the weather, but it wouldn't come. It was the other who supplied the conventional observation.

"Corking night," said Renneker. "It looks like a fine day for the game to-morrow."

They were side by side now. Leonard wondered whether he should go on, maintaining his own pace, or slow down and suit his steps to Renneker's. It was sort of embarrassing, he thought. He agreed about the weather and Renneker spoke again.

"I suppose you're trying to walk them off," he said.

"Walk them off?" echoed Leonard. There seemed nothing to do save fall in step with the other.

"Nerves," explained Renneker. "Guess that's what I'm doing myself."

"Oh," said Leonard a bit sheepishly. "Yes, I—I guess I am. At least, I suppose it's nerves. Slim wanted me to go to the mass meeting, but I sort of hated being with that howling mob to-night."

"Exactly." They had reached the corner and with one consent turned now and went slowly along Academy street. "Funny how panicky you can get the night before a game," mused Renneker.

Leonard laughed incredulously. "I can't imagine you ever getting like that," he said.

"I do, though," replied the other in his even voice. "Always have. Of course, it's absolute rot, because you know that just as soon as the whistle blows you're going to be perfectly all right again."

"Wish I knew that," answered Leonard.

"You do, only you can't remember it." There was a silence then while Leonard tried to digest that statement. Then Renneker went on. "It's rather absurd for me to be feeling jumpy to-night, for I'm not going to play. Must be just habit, I suppose. Queer."

"I wish you were going to play," said Leonard with such evident sincerity that Renneker looked down curiously at him.

"You do? I shouldn't think you would." He laughed shortly. "You might be out of it yourself if I did, Grant."

"I know, but—well, it's just sort of an accident with me, while you really belong, Renneker. I don't suppose that sounds very clear."

"Oh, yes. Well, I guess you'll get on all right, Grant. If you do, it won't matter much about me. Of course, I am disappointed, hang it! The whole silly thing is so—so—" He seemed almost on the point of becoming agitated, which was perhaps why he stopped abruptly. After a moment he continued with a note of amusement. "Really, Grant, I don't know why I'm chattering to you like this. I don't believe we ever spoke before yesterday. It must be the nerves!"

"Oh, yes, we have," answered Leonard. "Spoken, I mean. We came up from the station together that first day."

"We did?" Renneker seemed to be searching his memory. "Oh, then you were that chap in the taxi. I'd forgotten."

Leonard believed it. "I guess talking sort of does a fellow good," he said after a moment. "When he's jumpy, I mean."

"I dare say." There was silence again while they came to the main gate and passed it unheedingly. Across Academy street the light in Coach Cade's front room was turned down. "I suppose he's at the meeting," said Renneker. "Sort of a decent chap, Cade."

"Yes," agreed Leonard, "I think so. All the fellows seem to like him."

"Including me?" asked Renneker dryly.

"Why, I don't know," stammered Leonard. "Yes, I guess so. It wasn't his fault, after all, was it? I mean I suppose he had to do it."

"Do what?" asked Renneker, peering down.

"Why," floundered Leonard, "I mean he had to—to do his duty. Stick to rules, you know. He wasn't—"

"Then you think it was Johnny who put me off?"

Leonard pulled up with a start. He wasn't supposed to know a thing, and here he had been giving himself away. He sought for a way out. Renneker broke the silence.

"Look here, Grant, I don't get this at all. Has Mr. Cade been talking?"

"No, not to me, at any rate."

"Well, somebody has," pursued Renneker grimly. "What have you heard, Grant? I wish you'd tell me."

After an instant's hesitation Leonard did so. Renneker listened in silence. "None of us have breathed a word of it," concluded the speaker earnestly. "Only Carnochan, and he was sore because of that scrap."

"Scrap be blowed," said Renneker. "There wasn't any scrap. Those fellows pushed into us and we had some words, merely joking. Then this fellow suddenly jumped at Reilly and tried to punch him and I stepped in the way and got the punch. I told him to behave and he jabbed at me again. Then I gave him one in the ribs. That's all there was to it. As far as we were concerned, the whole thing was a joke, but that crazy Irishman lost his temper, I guess."

"Yes," said Leonard, "I guess, from what Johnny says, that he's sort of hot-headed."

"Decidedly! And his hot-headedness has played the dickens with me, Grant. Look here, are you in a hurry? Let's sit down a minute. You've heard part of the story, and I'd like to tell you the rest of it. It'll do me good to get it off my chest to some one, I fancy."

They swung themselves to the top rail of the fence in the shadow between two lights and Renneker went on.

"This is confidential, Grant. I'd rather you didn't say anything about it to any one, if you don't mind. It might make worse trouble if it got around. Thanks. Now, let's see. I think I'd better start at the beginning. I dare say you've heard that I got a bit of a reputation at

Castle City High as a guard. We have pretty good teams there, and we generally manage to lick about every one we go up against. I don't believe I was much better than half a dozen other chaps on our team, last year or the year before, but it sort of got around that I was good and the New York papers played me up. There's a fellow named Cravath who lives in my town and he went to school here at Alton. Last summer he got after me. Told me about Alton and how much more of a chance there was for me here. I liked the high school well enough, but I'd always had an idea that I'd prefer a prep school. Besides, when it comes to going to college it's a help if you go up from a well-known school like Alton. We haven't much money; the family I mean. Father used to be very well off some six or eight years ago, and we grew up rather free-handed, us kids. Then he lost it. Quite a spectacular bust-up, Grant, but it wouldn't interest you. What I'm getting at is that when it came to a question of coming here for two years the lot of us had to do some figuring.

"There are three of us; George, who is the oldest—two years older than me—Grace, who comes in between, and me. George was starting college this fall, and Grace is in school in New York. So there wasn't an awful lot of money for me, you see. Oh, well, that hasn't much to do with it. I'm making a beastly long story of this. Anyway, father managed to get hold of some money and said I could come up here, although he wasn't very keen about it, I fancy. And I came. I knew that the reason Dick Cravath was so anxious to get me here was because I could play football, and I intended making good. But I haven't done it. Oh, I've played, but I haven't played the way I should, or the way I can, Grant. And I guess the main reason was because this thing's been hanging over my head all the time. I've been waiting for it to break ever since the day I came up from New York."

"Then," exclaimed Leonard, "you knew that—that Johnny McGrath— But you couldn't have!"

"No, all I knew was what I got from a pimply-faced fellow who sold papers and magazines on the train. I bought a magazine from him and he looked me over and winked. 'Say, I know you, all right,' he told me. 'You're Ralston. I saw you play in a game in New London.' I told him he was wrong, but he wouldn't have it that way. He told me all about the game. Even knew how much money the club there had paid me for playing first base. I let him talk, because I wanted to learn what he knew. When he told me I'd played against a team called the Crescents from this town I knew I was in for trouble. I was pretty sure that sooner or later some chap who had played with the Crescents would see me and recognize me. Well, I fancy that got on my mind, Grant. In fact, I know it did. I couldn't seem to play the way I played last year. Of course, I might have turned around when I got here that day and gone back, after getting that story from the train-boy, but—oh, well, you always trust to the off chance. I don't know now whether I'm sorry or not that I didn't turn back. I'm out of football this year, but I like the school, and I've met some nice fellows. I—don't know." Renneker's voice dwindled into silence.

Nine o'clock struck from a church tower. Leonard sat, none too comfortably, on the angular rail and puzzled. All through his narrative his companion had sounded an under note of resentment, as though Fate had dealt unjustly with him. Of course, it was hard luck to get dropped from the team as Renneker had, but after all he had no one to blame but himself. Leonard sought an answer to one of the features of the story that puzzled him.

"You didn't know the Crescents came from here, then?" he asked. "I mean the day you played against them at New London."

"What? Oh! No, I didn't know that, Grant, because, you see, I wasn't there."

"You weren't—where?" inquired Leonard blankly.

"At New London," replied Renneker calmly.

"Then how—" Leonard blinked at the other in the gloom. "But you've said you were! If you weren't at New London, how did you play first base for the—the Maple Leaf nine?"

"I didn't."

Leonard laughed flatly. "I guess I'm stupid," he said.

"I've got your promise that this goes no further?" asked Renneker. Leonard nodded vigorously. "All right. I didn't play on that team,

158

Grant. I couldn't. I'm no good at all at baseball. That was my brother."

"Your brother!" exclaimed Leonard.

"Yes. He looks like me, a whole lot like me, although if you saw us together you wouldn't be fooled long. He's two years older than I am, nearly three, and he's an inch taller but not quite so heavy. His name is George Ralston Renneker, Ralston after my mother's folks. That's why I knew what was up when the train boy put that name on me. George is—oh, he's all right, Grant, but he's a nut. Sort of crazy about some things. We've always been great pals, but I've bawled him out a thousand times. He hasn't any idea about the value of money and he keeps right on spending it just as if we still had it. When he gets flat and father won't come across he goes off and plays baseball or hockey or anything to get some coin. He can do just about anything fairly well, you see. I suppose it isn't always just the money, either, for he's nuts on all sorts of sports, and he has to keep going at something or bust. Once he rode in a steeplechase near home and got thrown and had a couple of ribs broken. There wasn't any money in it that time. He just did it for fun, for the adventure. I fancy he'd jump off the Woolworth Tower with an umbrella if there was enough money waiting him below! Sometimes he makes quite a lot of money. Once he drew down a hundred and fifty for a ten-round preliminary bout over in Philadelphia. He boxes rather better than he does anything, I fancy. He was the 'Trenton Kid' that night. Usually he goes under the name of George Ralston. He's a nut, Grant."

Leonard digested this remarkable information in silence for a moment. Then: "But if it wasn't you, Renneker," he exclaimed, "why did you let them drop you from the team? I don't see that."

"You will in a minute," answered the other patiently. "George is at—well, never mind the college; it's not more than a hundred miles from here. This is his first year. I dare say it will be his last, too, for he doesn't stick long. He went to three schools. But I don't want him to get in trouble if I can help it. He's out for baseball and track already, and he will probably try hockey, too. If this thing got around he'd be dished, and it would mean a lot more to him than it did to me. Of course, you can say that I'm compounding a felony or

159

something, but I don't care if you do. I realize that George hasn't any right to take part in athletics at his college, but that's between him and his own conscience. I'm not going to be the one to queer him. I've known all along that when this thing broke it would be up to me to be the goat. Well, it did. And I am."

Leonard shook his head. "It isn't right, though, Renneker. It puts you out of football—and everything else, for that matter—this year and next. Why, even when you go up to college this thing will follow you, I guess!"

"Well, I'm rather expecting that by next fall I can tell the truth," answered Renneker. "It isn't likely that poor old George will last more than his freshman year without getting found out. If they have something else on him one more thing won't matter, I guess. Anyway, I mean to keep in training on the chance of it."

"Does he know about it?" asked Leonard presently. "That you're taking the blame for this and have lost your place on the team?"

"Oh, no. What's the use of worrying him about it? He'd be just idiot enough to give the snap away and spoil his own fun."

"Serve him right," said Leonard indignantly. "I think it's a rotten shame that you've got to suffer for his—his misdoings!"

"Oh, well, it isn't as bad as that. I guess I've groused a good deal, Grant, but, after all, I'm glad to do it for the old coot. He'd do anything in the world for me without batting an eye-lid. Besides, I'm feeling quite a lot better now that I've unburdened my mind to some one. Talk does help a lot sometimes, and I fancy Providence must have sent you forth to-night to hear my tale of woe. Much obliged, really, for being so patient, my dear chap."

"Don't be an ass," begged Leonard. Half an hour before he would have gasped at the idea of inferring that Renneker was an ass, but just now it didn't even occur to him. "I was glad to listen. Just the same, Renneker, you are acting wrong in this business. I suppose I can't convince you—"

"Afraid not, Grant."

"—but it's a fact, just the same. Aside from everything else, you owe something to the team and the School, and you're letting them both down when you do this thing. You—you're endangering to-morrow's game, and—"

"I've thought of all that, Grant, and I don't agree with you. My own people come before the School or the team—"

"But, Great Scott," interrupted Leonard impatiently, "in this case your own people, your brother, I mean, is in the wrong! You're helping him to get away with something that isn't—"

"Absolutely, but when it *is* your brother that doesn't count much with you."

"It ought to," muttered Leonard.

"Possibly, but it doesn't. As for to-morrow's game, Grant, I'm absolutely sincere when I say that I believe you will do just as well as I'd have done."

"That's nonsense," Leonard protested.

"No, it isn't, really. I haven't been playing much of a game this fall. I've just managed to keep my position, and that's about all. Johnny Cade has been on the point of dropping me into the subs lots of times. I've seen it and I've had to act haughty and pull a bluff to keep him from doing it."

"That's all right," persisted the younger boy doggedly, "but you say yourself that was because this business was hanging over you. Well, it isn't hanging over you any longer, and there's no reason why you shouldn't play to-morrow as well as you've ever played. Now, isn't that so?"

"My dear chap," replied Renneker, smoothly evasive, "you ought to be a prosecuting attorney or something. I say, what time is it getting to be? You fellows are supposed to be in hall by nine-thirty."

"It isn't that yet," answered Leonard. But he slid down from the fence and fell into step beside the other. He tried very hard to think of something that would persuade Renneker out of this pig-headed, idiotic course. He grudgingly admired the big fellow for what he had done. It was chivalrous and generous and all that sort of thing, this

161

business of being the goat for Brother George, but Leonard didn't know Brother George and he couldn't summon any sympathy for him. When he did speak again they were well up the broad path to Academy Hall, and what he said wasn't at all what he had sought for.

"I do wish you'd think this over to-night, Renneker," he pleaded.

"My dear chap," replied the other very patiently and kindly, "you mustn't think any more about it. It's all settled, and there's no harm done. If you keep on, you know, you'll make me sorry I confided in you." Renneker laughed softly.

"I don't care," persisted Leonard weakly. "It's a rotten shame!" Then an idea came to him. "Look here," he exclaimed, "what's to keep me from telling Johnny?"

"Not a thing," was the cool response, "except your promise not to."

Leonard growled inarticulately.

In front of Academy they parted, Renneker to seek his room in Upton, and Leonard to take the other direction. The mass meeting was over and the fellows were pouring out from Memorial, still noisily enthusiastic. "Well, I hope I haven't added to your nerves, Grant," said Renneker. "Just remember that when the whistle blows you won't have any, and that having them now consequently doesn't matter one iota. That may help. I'm in Upton, you know; Number 9. Come in and see me some time, won't you? Good night."

"Good night," replied Leonard. He had difficulty making his voice sound disapproving, but he managed it after a fashion. Renneker laughed as he turned away.

"Try to forget my faults, Grant," he called back, "and think only of my many virtues!"

Upstairs in Number 12 Slim was displaying a hurt expression. He had left the meeting when it was no more than half over to hurry back and stroke the other's head, he explained, and here the other was gallivanting around the campus! Leonard apologized. He did not, however, mention Renneker. Why, he couldn't have told.

CHAPTER XXII
BEFORE THE BATTLE

The squad, thirty-one in all, including coaches, managers, trainer and rubbers, left Alton the next forenoon at a little after ten o'clock. About every one else around the academy took the train that left at twelve-eight, partaking of an early and hurried dinner at half-past eleven. As very few were at all concerned with food just then, being much too excited, no one missed the train.

Unexpectedly, Leonard had slept exceedingly sound and for a full eight hours and a half. He had lain awake no later than eleven, while Slim, though more of a veteran, had heard midnight strike, as he aggrievedly proclaimed in the morning. Possibly it was that conversation with Gordon Renneker that was to be credited with Leonard's early and sound slumber, for Renneker's affairs had driven all thoughts of Leonard's from the latter's mind, and instead of being nervous and jumpy he had been merely impatient and indignant—and sometimes admiring—and had made himself sleepy trying to think up some way of inducing Renneker to stop being a Don Quixote and act like a rational human being. He hadn't solved his problem, but he had sent himself to sleep.

Renneker, having worked hard if briefly at coaching the linemen, went along with the squad. So, too, did Mr. Fadden, who, having wrestled with the problem of the second team for some five weeks, was now in position to act, in an advisory capacity, as Mr. Cade's assistant. In the hustle for seats in the special car that had been tacked onto the long train for the accommodation of the team, Leonard and his suit-case got tucked into a corner of a seat near the rear door, escape, had he desired it, being prevented by the generous bulk of Jim Newton. He and Jim talked a little, but the center had supplied himself with a New York morning paper at the station and was soon deep in a frowning perusal of the football news. That Renneker would change his mind, make a clean breast of everything and come back into the fold was something Leonard had hoped for up to the last moment of leaving school. But he hadn't done anything of the sort. That was proved by the fact that he carried no bag. You couldn't quite vision Gordon Renneker facing Kenly Hall on the football gridiron in an immaculate suit of blue serge, a pale yellow shirt and black-and-white sport shoes! So Leonard's hopes went glimmering, and when Renneker, passing him on the platform, nodded and said, "Hi, old chap!" Leonard just grunted and scowled his disappointment.

The day was a lot colder than the evening had presaged, but it was fair and there were few clouds in the very blue sky. The car, like most railway cars, was incapable of compromise in the matter of temperature. Since it was not freezing cold it was tropically hot. Squeezed in there by the steam pipes, with Jim Newton overflowing on him, Leonard suffered as long as possible and then forced a way past the grunting Newton and sought the water tank. Of course the water was close to the temperature of the car, but that was to be expected. At least, it was wet. After two drinks from the razor-like edge of a paper cup that was enough to make one long for the unhygienic days of old, he went forward, resisting the blandishments of those who would have detained him, and passed into the car ahead. There were plenty of seats here, and, although that may have been just his imagination, the car seemed cooler by several degrees. It wasn't until he had slammed the door behind him that he saw Gordon Renneker in the first seat at the left. Renneker looked up, nodded and moved slightly closer to the window. Of course, Leonard reflected, he thinks I saw him come in here and have followed him on purpose. Well, I'll show him!

"Hello," he said aloud, taking the seat after a moment of seeming indecision, "I didn't know you were in here. It got so hot back there that I had to get out."

"I came in here," replied Renneker, "because Mr. Fadden insisted on telling me how much better football was played in his day. It seems, Grant, that ten or twenty years ago every team consisted of eleven Olympians. Every man Jack was a star of the first magnitude and a Prince among fellows. Fadden says so. Why, every blessed one of the chaps who played on his team in college is to-day either President of the United States or president of one of the big railroad systems. Every one, that is, except Fadden. I don't know what happened to him. He seems to have been the only mediocre chap in the bunch. I must ask him about that some time," Renneker ended musingly.

Leonard laughed in spite of himself. He hadn't wanted to laugh. He had wanted to make Renneker understand clearly that he was still as strongly disapproving of his conduct as ever. But Renneker was sort of different to-day. He was lighter-hearted and even facetious, it appeared. Leonard had to thaw. They talked about the game for a few minutes, but neither introduced the subject of last evening's talk until, as though suddenly reminded, Renneker said: "By the way, Grant, remember what we were talking about last night? What I was, that is!" He laughed gently and put a hand into a pocket of his coat. "Well, I want you to read this. It's rather a joke on me, and you'll probably enjoy it hugely. This came by this morning's mail."

He produced an envelope from his pocket and took forth a single sheet of twice-folded paper and handed it to Leonard. "Read it," he said. Leonard opened it and saw, at the top, the name, in none too modest characters, of a New York hotel. Then he read:

"DEAR GORDIE:

"Well, we're off again, old timer. Came down last night and leave in about twenty minutes for Louisiana. Saved the faculty the trouble of bouncing me. It was only an innocent childish prank, but you know how faculties are. Four of our crowd didn't like the show at the theatre and quit it cold after the first act. There was a car outside that looked good, and the fellow who belonged to it hadn't anchored it or locked it or anything. So we thought we'd take a little spin and come back before the show was over. How, I ask you, were we to know that the owner couldn't stand the show either? Well, he came out and couldn't find his bus and squealed to the police and they telephoned all around and a cop on a motor cycle pulled us in about six miles out and took us back to the station. If the guy had been the right sort it would have been O.K., but he was a sour-faced pill without an ounce of compassion and insisted on making a charge against us. We got bail all right, and yesterday morning the trifling matter was settled on a money basis, but the dickens of it was that faculty got hep and we had our rather and chose to resign instead of getting fired. Townsend's father has a rice farm or plantation or something in Louisiana and he's going to get me a job. There'll be lots of riding, he says, and I guess it'll keep me going until I can look around. We're starting down there at eleven-thirty. I'll write when I reach the place and send the address. I've forgotten the name of the town and Jim's out getting tickets. I've written to Dad, but you might drop him a line, too, old timer. You know what to say, you were always the diplomat of the family. I'll be fixed for coin, so he won't have to worry about that. Hope everything is hunky with you, dear old pal.

> "Your aff. brother,
> "GEORGE."

Leonard returned the epistle, staring at Renneker blankly. The latter laughed. "I might have known he couldn't stick," he said. "It's just like the crazy coot to have it happen a week too late, too. If he'd skipped Thursday before last instead of this Thursday—" Renneker shook his head in comic resignation.

"But—but—but," stammered Leonard, "you can play to-day, can't you? All you've got to do is tell Mr. Cade!"

"My dear chap," remonstrated the other, "one doesn't upset the arrangements at the last moment. Oh, I did consider it, but, pshaw, what would be the good? Everything's fixed and if I butted in I'd just muddle things horribly. Besides, I really haven't the courage to try to explain it all in the brief time remaining. But, honest, Grant, it is a sort of a ghastly joke, isn't it? Why don't you laugh, you sober-face? I thought it would amuse you!"

Leonard viewed him scathingly. "Honest, Renneker," he replied with slow and painstaking enunciation, "you give me an acute pain!"

Renneker smiled more broadly. "Good boy! Speak your mind! However, if you'll stop being peeved and think a minute you'll see that it wouldn't do to upset Johnny's apple-cart at this late hour. Besides, I haven't brought my togs, and couldn't play decently if I had. Why, I haven't practiced for a week, Grant."

"You don't need practice," responded Leonard earnestly. "A fellow like you—"

"The dickens I don't!" scoffed Renneker. "I'm as stiff as a crutch. Be a good fellow, Grant, and stop scolding." Renneker looked at the letter in his hand, returned it to its envelope and placed it back in his pocket with a smile of resignation. "Just plain nut," he said. "That's what he is."

Leonard, watching, was suddenly realizing that this new acquaintance of his was a very likeable chap and that, although he did feel thoroughly out of patience with him just now, he was getting to have a sort of affection for him. Of course he wouldn't have had Renneker suspect the fact for an instant, but there it was! The big fellow's story seemed to explain a good deal, such as, for instance, that the calm superiority affected by him had really been a blind to conceal the fact that he was secretly in a state of nervous apprehension, in short a colossal bluff that not even Coach Cade had had the nerve to call! It must have been, Leonard reflected sympathetically, rather a job to play good football and know that at any moment exposure might occur. And, after all, that letter of George Renneker's had rather won Leonard. Of course the fellow was an irresponsible, hair-brained ass, but, nevertheless, the reader had seemed to find something likeable in the writer of that amazing epistle, and he understood somewhat better why Gordon had felt it worth while to protect George even at the cost of his own undoing. He wasn't frowning any longer when Renneker looked back from a momentary inspection of the flying landscape beyond the car window. Renneker must have noted the change, for he asked:

"Decided to overlook my transgressions?"

Leonard nodded, smiling faintly. "Yes, although I still think you're all wrong. Let me tell you one thing, too. If—if"—he stumbled a little there—"if you're doing this because you think I'd be—be disappointed about not playing, Renneker, you can just quit it right now. I never expected to play in this game—anyhow, I haven't for a good while—and it won't mean a thing to me if I don't. So if that's it, or if that has anything to do with it—"

"My dear chap," replied Renneker soothingly, "when you know me better you'll realize that I'm not a Sir Launcelot or a—a Galahad. Rest quite easy."

It wasn't, though, a positive denial, and Leonard was by no means convinced. He looked doubtfully, even suspiciously at the somewhat quizzical countenance of the other and subsided. And then a trainman banged open a door and shouted "La-a-akeville! Lakeville!" and Leonard hurried back for his suit-case.

They went to the hotel for luncheon, walking up from the station and pretending they didn't know that they were objects of interest all the way along the five blocks. There remained the better part of an hour before the meal was to be served, and after depositing their bags in the room that was to serve them for dressing purposes, most of the party descended again to the street and set off to see the town. Slim claimed Leonard as his companion, but Leonard begged off rather mysteriously and Slim set out a trifle huffily in company with Appel and Menge. Leonard then set out to find Mr. Cade, and after several unsuccessful inquiries had failed to discover that gentleman, Tod Tenney came skipping down the stairs and, his escape blocked by Leonard, revealed the fact that Mr. Cade and Mr. Fadden were in Room 17. Leonard, likewise scorning the snail-like elevator, climbed the stairs and found the room. Mr. Cade's voice answered his knock. The coach and his associate were sitting in straight-back chairs in front of a long window, their feet on the sill and pipes going busily. Mr. Fadden looked around, waving the smoke clouds from before him with the newspaper he held, and said sotto voce: "One of the boys, Cade."

"Can I speak to you a moment, sir?" asked Leonard.

Mr. Cade's feet came down from the sill with a bang and he swung around. "Oh, hello, Grant! Why, certainly. Anything wrong?"

"No, sir. It's about—" He hesitated and glanced dubiously at Mr. Fadden.

"Oh, that's all right," laughed Mr. Cade. "You can speak before Mr. Fadden. Pull up that chair and sit down first."

Leonard obeyed, occupying, however, only some six inches of the chair's surface. "It's about Gordon Renneker, sir," he began again.

"Renneker?" The coach looked interested at once. "What about Renneker, Grant?"

"Well—" Leonard stopped and started anew: "Wouldn't it help us a lot, Mr. Cade, if he played to-day?"

"Probably, but I thought it was understood that Renneker was—er—out of football. What's on your mind?"

"I can't explain it very well," answered Leonard, "because I promised not to speak about—about part of it. That makes it—difficult." He looked at Mr. Cade and then at Mr. Fadden as though seeking assistance. Mr. Cade frowned perplexedly.

"I'm afraid I can't help you, Grant, for I don't know what you're trying to get at. If you're troubled about Renneker not playing, why, I'll have to tell you that there isn't anything you can do about that. We're looking for you to see to it that he isn't missed, Grant. And we think you can do it."

Leonard shook his head. "That isn't it, sir. I know something that I can't tell, because I promised not to." He stopped and strove to arrange matters in his mind. He wished he had composed a statement before coming. Regarding all that Renneker had revealed to him last evening his lips were sealed. It was only about what had transpired this morning that he was not sworn to silence. It was, though, hard to keep the two apart, and he didn't want to break his promise. Mr. Cade, watching him intently, waited in patience. Mr. Fadden puffed hard at his pipe, silently friendly. Leonard rushed the hurdle.

"If you'll tell Renneker that you want to read a letter he received this morning, sir," he blurted, "you'll understand."

"Tell him I want to read a letter he received?" repeated the coach in puzzled tones. "But why should I, Grant?"

"Why, because when you do read it, and Renneker has explained it, you—he—why, sir, he can play this afternoon!"

"Oh!" said Mr. Cade thoughtfully. After an instant he said: "Look here, Grant, you must know a whole lot about this business of Renneker's."

Leonard nodded. "Yes, sir, I know all about it. I—I knew about it before you did."

The coach gazed at him curiously, opened his lips as if to speak, closed them again and glanced questioningly at Mr. Fadden.

"Better see Renneker and get it cleared up," said the second team coach oracularly. "Where there's so much smoke there must be some fire. Let's get at it."

"All right." He turned to Leonard again. "I suppose you realize that if Renneker plays right guard to-day you don't, Grant. At least, not long, probably."

"Yes, sir, but Renneker's a lot better than I am, and if he can play it doesn't matter about me, does it?"

"H'm, no, I suppose it doesn't. Well, I'm much obliged to you, my boy. Whether anything comes of this or doesn't, I quite understand that you've tried to help us. Do you know where Renneker is just now?"

"No, sir, not exactly. He went out right after we reached the hotel. I—I guess I could find him."

"Do it, will you? Tell him—tell him whatever you think best. You know more about this mystery than we do. Only see that he gets here right away. Thanks, Grant."

"Could I tell him that you and Mr. Fadden want to see him to talk to him about the game?" asked Leonard. "If he suspected anything he might not want to come."

"The mystery deepens!" sighed Mr. Cade. "But tell him that by all means. It's totally and literally true. Just see that he comes a-running!"

Lakeville was in gala attire. Cherry-and-black pennants and bunting adorned the store windows, and beyond the casement of the town's principal haberdasher the appropriate colors were massed in a display of neckties and mufflers. Here and there the rival hues of gray-and-gold were shown, but it was not until the arrival of the Alton rooters that Lakeville became noticeably leavened with the brighter tints. Leonard encountered Billy Wells and Sam Butler just outside the hotel, but neither of them had seen Gordon Renneker lately, and Leonard went on up the busy street on his quest. He discovered Slim and three others admiring the contents of a bake shop window and bore Slim away with him.

"We've got to find Renneker," he announced anxiously.

"I don't see why," objected Slim. "I'm going to be just as happy, General, if I never set eyes on him again."

"Dry up and come on. Mr. Cade wants him right off."

"Mr. Cade has strange fancies," murmured Slim, but he accelerated his steps. "Been over to the school grounds?"

"No, I haven't had time. Isn't that—no, it isn't. It did look like him, back-to."

"It looks like him front-to," replied Slim, "except that this guy is about forty-five and has different features and has lost some of his hair and wears glasses—"

"Oh, for the love of mud, shut up, Slim! And do look around, can't you? I tell you this is important."

"I do wish I could feel it so," said Slim exasperatingly, "but I just can't get up any enthusiasm for the chase. Besides, it's getting perilously close to chow time, and we're going in the wrong direction and—"

"There he is!" Leonard left Slim abruptly and darted across the street, narrowly escaping the ignominy of being run down by a rattling flivver adorned with cherry-and-black pennants. Gordon Renneker had just emerged from a doorway above which hung a black-and-gold sign announcing "Olympic Lunch Room—Good Eats," and still held in one hand the larger part of a cheese sandwich.

"Say, what the—" Renneker stared in amazement from Leonard to the sandwich now lying in unappetizing fragments on the sidewalk.

"Awfully sorry," panted Leonard, "but you're wanted at the hotel right away. Room 17."

"I'm wanted? What for?" Leonard saw suspicion creeping into Renneker's eyes.

"Mr. Cade and Mr. Fadden," he answered quickly and glibly. "They told me to tell you they wanted to see you about the game right away."

"Flattering," said Renneker. "Oh, all right. Wait till I get another sandwich—"

"You mustn't," declared Leonard. "It's almost lunch time, and they're waiting for you, and they'll be mad if you don't come quick!" He pulled Renneker away from the lunch room doorway and guided him rapidly toward the hotel. From across the street a perplexed and insulted Slim watched them disappear.

"Abandoned!" he muttered. "Adrift in a strange and cruel city! Heaven help me!"

CHAPTER XXIII
"FIFTY-FIFTY!"

Leonard sat on the bench on the Alton side of the field and watched the kickers at work. There had been a good ten minutes of signal drill for both squads and now only the punters and drop-kickers remained on the gridiron. The game was about to start. Across the field the Kenly Hall sections were cheering loudly each member of their team in turn. The officials were talking earnestly on the sideline. Something white fluttered across Leonard's shoulder from the stand above and behind him and settled at his feet. He stooped and picked it up. It proved to be the two middle pages of the official program. He looked around to see if any one would claim it. But no one did and he settled back and regarded the thing. On each page, where they had faced each other before they had torn loose, were the line-ups of the teams, Alton to the left, Kenly Hall to the right, each boxed in by advertisements of local enterprises: "White Swan Laundry—Special Rates to Academy Men—You Can't Go Wrong, Fellows!" "Bell and Falk, Photographers to All Classes Since 1912." "Lakeville Pressing Club—Best and Quickest Service in the City—" Leonard's attention wandered to the column of names in the center of the page. "Alton," he read. "Staples, left end; Butler, left tackle; Stimson, left guard; Newton, center; Grant, right guard; Wells, right tackle; Emerson, Capt., right end; Appel, quarterback; Menge, left halfback; Reilly, right halfback; Greenwood, fullback."

His gaze crossed to the opposite list: "Hanley, left end; Pope, left tackle; Tinkner, left guard; Henderson, center—" Interest waned, and he returned to the first row of names; especially to the fifth from the top. This was the first time Leonard had ever seen his name in a regular program, to say nothing of one with a colored cover and costing fifteen cents, and he was pardonably thrilled. It was, he reflected, something to have your name down in the line-up, even if you didn't play!

And Leonard wasn't going to play; at least, not much. He felt pretty confident of getting into the game long enough to secure his letter, and, if luck was with him, he might even play for five minutes or ten, supposing Renneker or Stimson failed to last. But, in spite of the official program, Renneker was right guard to-day and not Grant.

Leonard didn't know what had taken place in Room 17 just before luncheon, what arguments Mr. Cade had used, but he did know that Renneker had capitulated. He hadn't spoken to Renneker since, for they had sat at different tables at luncheon and afterwards all had been hurry and bustle, with some of the fellows riding to the field in jitneys and others walking. Leonard had walked, with Slim and Perry Stimson and Red Reilly. The conversation had been mostly about Renneker, for that youth had appeared a few moments before in a football costume of borrowed togs and Manager Tenney had spread the joyous news that the big fellow was to play. Stimson and Reilly did most of the speculating, for Slim, although clearly puzzled, knew so much that he was afraid to discuss the matter lest he say too much, and Leonard kept discreetly silent and was supposed by the others to be too disappointed to find words. Slim evidently suspected Leonard of being in the know, but there was no chance to charge him with it. Stimson and Reilly were much pleased by the reinstatement of Renneker, although they charitably strove to disguise the fact out of sympathy for Leonard.

Only once had Leonard come face to face with Gordon Renneker, and then it was in the crowded lobby of the hotel. Leonard's look of mingled defiance and apology had been answered by an eloquent shrug of Renneker's broad shoulders and a hopeless shake of the head. But the big fellow wasn't really angry, and Leonard was glad of that. Leonard had had several qualms of conscience since that visit to Room 17, and it had required much argument to convince himself that he had not, after all, violated a confidence.

Across the sunlit field the Kenly Hall band of seven pieces broke into sound again, and a drum boomed loudly and a cornet blared and the cheering section was off on a ribald song that ended with:

"And the foe turned Gray when it came to pass
What looked like Gold was only brass!"

The gridiron emptied. From the further side-line a man in a white sweater advanced with a khaki-clad youth whose stockings were ringed with cherry-red and black. Captain Emerson walked out and

174

met them. The rival leaders shook hands. A silver coin caught the sunlight as it spun aloft and dropped to the turf. Captain Growe, of Kenly, pointed toward the west goal and the little group broke up. A minute later the teams were in place and the cheering was stilled. The referee's voice floated across on the northerly breeze:

"Are you ready, Captain Emerson?... Ready, Captain Growe?"

A whistle piped and Kenly kicked off at two minutes past two.

Twenty-five minutes and some seconds later, when the first period ended, several facts had become apparent to Leonard, watching unblinkingly from the bench. One was that Alton and Kenly were about as evenly matched in power and skill as any two teams could be. Another was that, whichever won, the final score was going to be very small. And the third was that Gordon Renneker was playing the kind of football to-day that had won him a place on the All-Scholastic Team!

With the wind, scarcely more than a strong breeze, behind her in that first quarter, Kenly played a kicking game. But with the rival ends as closely matched as they were to-day her punts won her little advantage. Cricket Menge and Bee Appel always ran them back for fair distances before they were thrown, and Joe Greenwood, returning the punts, got almost equal ground. Each team tried out the opposing line systematically without discovering any especially weak places. Each team found that running the ends was no certain way to gain. The ball changed hands again and again, hovering over the middle of the field. Twice Alton made her first down and twice Kenly did the same. Alton was penalized once for holding and Kenly was set back twice for off-side. Each team made two attempts at forward-passing and each failed to gain a foot by that method. When the quarter ended honors were even.

The second period started out to be a duplicate of the first. There was a heart-thrilling moment when Dill, of Kenly, made the first real run of the day by leaking past Captain Emerson and eluding Reilly and placing the pigskin eleven yards nearer the Alton goal. Yet, to counter that, the Kenly attack was thrice spilled before it got well started and the Cherry-and-Black was forced to punt again. Menge was hurt in a tackle and Kendall took his place. Alton braced near her thirty-one yards and carried the ball across the center line, concentrating on the left of the enemy's line and alternating with Kendall and Greenwood. But just inside Kenly territory the advance petered out and a long forward to Slim Staples grounded and Kendall punted over the goal-line.

A few minutes later Alton again got the pigskin on her forty-seven and began a punting game. With the wind behind him, Kendall was good for something more than five yards better than the Kenly punter, and after four exchanges the wisdom of the switch was evident, for Alton found herself in possession of the ball on Kenly's thirty-eight yards, following a four yard run-back by Appel. An attack on left tackle netted a scant two yards, and on second down Kendall once more went back to kicking position. The play, however, proved a short heave over the line that Reilly couldn't reach. From the same formation Kendall tried to get around the left on a wide run but was forced out for no gain. With the ball too far over on the side of the field for an attempt at a goal, Greenwood took Kendall's place and Kenly covered her backfield for a punt. But Appel was crafty, the enemy had scattered her secondary defense and the unexpected happened. The ball went to Reilly, and Red dashed straight ahead through a comfortably wide hole opened for him by Renneker and Wells and put the pigskin down on the twenty-seven!

Pandemonium reigned on the south stands. Alton hoarsely demanded a touchdown and Gray-and-Gold pennants waved and fluttered. On the bench below, Leonard clenched his hands on his knees and watched with straining gaze. There was time out for Kenly and a fresh player went in at right half. Then Alton lined up again and Appel's shrill voice called the signal.

It was Kendall back once more, but Greenwood got the ball and dug through for something less than two yards. On the same play he got one more, placing the pigskin just over Kenly's twenty-five-yard line. Then a play designed for just such a situation, a play that had been practiced until it went as smoothly as a lot of oiled cogs, was called for. Kendall was still eight yards back, Appel knelt before him to take the ball from Newton and Kenly was on her toes to break through. And then something happened. One of the cogs slipped, perhaps. At all events, the ball never arose from Kendall's toe, and when the whistle blew the Alton quarterback was found at the bottom of the pile with the pigskin desperately clutched in his arms. The perfect play had gone agley, and instead of a deceptive end run by quarter, with fullback swinging at empty air, it was fourth down for a six yard loss!

On the same play he got one more

And then, while the Alton stands were blankly confronting the sudden change in affairs, while Leonard was heaving a sigh that had seemed to come from the very cleats of his shoes, Appel was piping his signal again, undismayed, as it seemed by the misfortune. Now it was Captain Emerson back, with Kenly somehow suspecting a forward-pass instead of the threatened drop-kick. Well, a drop-kick from somewhere around the thirty-seven yards, even with a breeze behind the kicker, did look fishy. And yet that is just what followed. If Jim Newton had been at fault before—and he may not have been, for all I know—he was perfect now. The ball went back breast-high, was dropped leisurely and sped off and up and over! And Alton had scored at last and some four hundred wearers of the Gray-and-Gold became hysterically joyful!

The half ended almost directly after that, with the score-board bearing a single numeral still, a "3" following the word "Alton."

Leonard went back to the dressing room with the others and sat around and listened and talked and was very excited and jubilant. Slim had a beautiful swelled lip and couldn't say much because he had to laugh every time he heard himself speak. Renneker waved a hand across the room at Leonard, but didn't come over. He had a nice broad ribbon of plaster under his right eye. Plaster, indeed, seemed quite a popular ornament. Mr. Cade talked for a minute while Tod Tenney stood at the door watching the hands on his watch. Leonard didn't hear what he said very well, but he cheered as loudly as any at the end. Then they piled out and started back.

Going along the bench, Leonard heard his name called and looked up the slanting stand to where a youth with a Gray-and-Gold flag draping his shoulders waved wildly. It was Johnny McGrath, Johnny very hoarse from much shouting, who was greeting him. Leonard grinned and waved back to him. Then, suddenly, the battle was on again, Kenly took the ball on the kick-off and ran it back to her twenty-eight before Billy Wells placed the runner on his head. Kenly smashed at the Alton right, stopped and formed again. Once more the teams crashed together. Kenly had made a yard. The whistle blew. Some one was still down. "Greenwood!" exclaimed Leonard's left-hand neighbor. Then: "No, Renneker, by gum!" Jake, the trainer, was bending over the injured player. A minute passed. Jake signaled to the bench. Mr. Cade jumped up and looked down the line until his eye met Leonard's. His head went back and Leonard disentangled himself from his blanket and obeyed the motion. On the field, Gordon Renneker, his head wobbling from side to side, was coming off between Jake and Rus Emerson.

"All right, Grant," said the coach. "You know what to do without my telling you. Go to it!"

There were cheers from the stand behind him as he sped on, cheers for Renneker and for Grant, short, snappy cheers that made a fellow tingle. Leonard eyed Renneker anxiously as he drew near the little group. The big fellow seemed to be just about all in, he thought. He didn't like the way his head lolled over on his shoulder, or those closed eyes of his. He hoped that— Then he stared. Renneker's eyes had opened as Leonard had come abreast, and then one of them had closed again in a most amazing wink! Leonard asked himself if he had imagined it. He turned his head to look back. Some one had taken Emerson's place, but Renneker's head still lolled and wobbled. He must have imagined that wink, and yet— No, by jiminy, he hadn't! He understood all at once. Renneker was faking! He had pretended an injury so that Leonard might have his place!

"Hey! Report to the referee, General!"

Appel's voice brought him out of his amazed thoughts. He looked for the white sweater, found it and slipped into the line. A whistle blew again and—well, after that he was very busy. The game went on, hard, gruelling. Alton advanced and retreated, Kenly won ground and lost it. The ball hurtled through the air, feet pounded the turf, bodies rasped together, tired lungs fought for breath and aching legs for strength. The third period came to an end, the score unchanged.

Leonard was playing better than he had ever played, better than he had thought himself capable of playing. His victories were not easily won, for his opponent was a big, hard-fighting fellow, but won they were. The right side of the Alton line was still holding firmly, and it continued to hold right up to those last few minutes of the game when the Cherry-and-Black, desperate, reinforced with fresh players, ground her way inexorably to the twenty-yard-line and, with Kenly throats imploring a touchdown, thrice threw her attack at the enemy line and was thrice repulsed almost under the shadow of the Alton goal.

The end was close then, the time-keeper had his eyes on his watch more often than on the game and all hope of a touchdown by rushing tactics was abandoned by the home team. Either a pass over the line or a field-goal must serve. Thus far Kenly's forward-passes had almost invariably failed, and this fact doubtless brought the decision to try for a tied score rather than a victory. At all events, Kenly placed her drop-kicker back, arranged her defenses and set the stage for the final act. The kicker was on the twenty-seven yards, no great distance now that the breeze had died away. The signal came, the ball shot back, the lines met.

Then it was that Leonard had his great moment. He went through, the first of his line to start when the ball was passed, the only one to penetrate that desperate wall in front of the kicker. Quite alone he charged, almost in the path of the ball. An enemy was met and evaded with a quick swing to the left. Hands clutched him, but too late. He was off his feet now, arms upstretched, leaping high in the air. Something swam toward him against the sunset light, brown and big, turning lazily in its flight. An arm swept into its path. Leonard was down in a writhing mass, had found his feet, was tossed aside. The battle was up the field now, back near the thirty-five-yard line. Leonard scrambled breathlessly up and staggered in the wake of the swarming players. A whistle blew and a voice, the referee's, was shouting:

"Alton's ball! First down!"

They were back in the hotel, the cheering and the tumult left behind for the while. The dressing room was crowded, full of confusion and excitement. Every one was talking, laughing, shouting at once. A wonderful sense of complete happiness held Leonard as he tugged at his laces. Just then it seemed as though nothing could ever possibly happen that would matter one bit. They had beaten Kenly Hall! And he had helped! Fellows were bumping into him, fairly walking over him, but he didn't mind. He didn't mind even when some one placed a big hand at the back of his head and bore down until it hurt. He looked up when he could, though. It was Gordon Renneker.

Leonard sought for words, beautiful, big, round, insulting words, but the best he could do was only:

"You—you blamed old faker!"

Renneker rumpled Leonard's damp hair rudely, grinning down.

"Fifty-fifty," he said.

THE END

This Isn't All!

Would you like to know what became of the good friends you have made in this book?

Would you like to read other stories continuing their adventures and experiences, or other books quite as entertaining by the same author?

On the *reverse side* of the wrapper which comes with this book, you will find a wonderful list of stories which you can buy at the same store where you got this book.

Don't throw away the Wrapper

Use it as a handy catalog of the books you want some day to have. But in case you do mislay it, write to the Publishers for a complete catalog.

Football and Baseball Stories

Durably Bound. Illustrated. Colored Wrappers.
Every Volume Complete in Itself.

The Ralph Henry Barbour Books for Boys

In these up-to-the-minute, spirited genuine stories of boy life there is something which will appeal to every boy with the love of manliness, cleanness and sportsmanship in his heart.

LEFT END EDWARDS

LEFT TACKLE THAYER

LEFT GUARD GILBERT

CENTER RUSH ROWLAND

FULLBACK FOSTER

LEFT HALF HARMON

RIGHT END EMERSON

RIGHT GUARD GRANT

QUARTERBACK BATES

RIGHT TACKLE TODD

RIGHT HALF HOLLINS

The Christy Mathewson Books for Boys

Every boy wants to know how to play ball in the fairest and squarest way. These books about boys and baseball are full of wholesome and manly interest and information.

PITCHER POLLOCK

CATCHER CRAIG

FIRST BASE FAULKNER

SECOND BASE SLOAN

PITCHING IN A PINCH

THIRD BASE THATCHER, By Everett Scott

GROSSET & DUNLAP, *Publishers*, NEW YORK

THE TOM SLADE BOOKS

By PERCY KEESE FITZHUGH

Author of "Roy Blakeley," "Pee-wee Harris," "Westy Martin," Etc.

Illustrated. Individual Picture Wrappers in Colors.
Every Volume Complete in Itself.

"Let your boy grow up with Tom Slade," is a suggestion which thousands of parents have followed during the past, with the result that the TOM SLADE BOOKS are the most popular boys' books published today. They take Tom Slade through a series of typical boy adventures through his tenderfoot days as a scout, through his gallant days as an American doughboy in France, back to his old patrol and the old camp ground at Black Lake, and so on.

TOM SLADE, BOY SCOUT

TOM SLADE AT TEMPLE CAMP

TOM SLADE ON THE RIVER

TOM SLADE WITH THE COLORS

TOM SLADE ON A TRANSPORT

TOM SLADE WITH THE BOYS OVER THERE

TOM SLADE, MOTORCYCLE DISPATCH BEARER

TOM SLADE WITH THE FLYING CORPS

TOM SLADE AT BLACK LAKE

TOM SLADE ON MYSTERY TRAIL

TOM SLADE'S DOUBLE DARE

TOM SLADE ON OVERLOOK MOUNTAIN

TOM SLADE PICKS A WINNER

TOM SLADE AT BEAR MOUNTAIN

TOM SLADE: FOREST RANGER

TOM SLADE IN THE NORTH WOODS

GROSSET & DUNLAP, *Publishers*, NEW YORK

THE ROY BLAKELEY BOOKS

By PERCY KEESE FITZHUGH

Author of "Tom Slade," "Pee-wee Harris," "Westy Martin," Etc.

Illustrated. Picture Wrappers in Color.
Every Volume Complete in Itself.

In the character and adventures of Roy Blakeley are typified the very essence of Boy life. He is a real boy, as real as Huck Finn and Tom Sawyer. He is the moving spirit of the troop of Scouts of which he is a member, and the average boy has to go only a little way in the first book before Roy is the best friend he ever had, and he is willing to part with his best treasure to get the next book in the series.

ROY BLAKELEY

ROY BLAKELEY'S ADVENTURES IN CAMP

ROY BLAKELEY, PATHFINDER

ROY BLAKELEY'S CAMP ON WHEELS

ROY BLAKELEY'S SILVER FOX PATROL

ROY BLAKELEY'S MOTOR CARAVAN

ROY BLAKELEY, LOST, STRAYED OR STOLEN

ROY BLAKELEY'S BEE-LINE HIKE

ROY BLAKELEY AT THE HAUNTED CAMP

ROY BLAKELEY'S FUNNY BONE HIKE

ROY BLAKELEY'S TANGLED TRAIL

ROY BLAKELEY ON THE MOHAWK TRAIL

ROY BLAKELEY'S ELASTIC HIKE

ROY BLAKELEY'S ROUNDABOUT HIKE

GROSSET & DUNLAP, *Publishers*, NEW YORK

THE PEE-WEE HARRIS BOOKS

By PERCY KEESE FITZHUGH

Author of "Tom Slade," "Roy Blakeley," "Westy Martin," Etc.

Illustrated. Individual Picture Wrappers in Color.
Every Volume Complete in Itself.

All readers of the Tom Slade and the Roy Blakeley books are acquainted with Pee-wee Harris. These stories record the true facts concerning his size (what there is of it) and his heroism (such as it is), his voice, his clothes, his appetite, his friends, his enemies, his victims. Together with the thrilling narrative of how he foiled, baffled, circumvented and triumphed over everything and everybody (except where he failed) and how even when he failed he succeeded. The whole recorded in a series of screams and told with neither muffler nor cut-out.

PEE-WEE HARRIS

PEE-WEE HARRIS ON THE TRAIL

PEE-WEE HARRIS IN CAMP

PEE-WEE HARRIS IN LUCK

PEE-WEE HARRIS ADRIFT

PEE-WEE HARRIS F. O. B. BRIDGEBORO

PEE-WEE HARRIS FIXER

PEE-WEE HARRIS: AS GOOD AS HIS WORD

PEE-WEE HARRIS: MAYOR FOR A DAY

PEE-WEE HARRIS AND THE SUNKEN TREASURE

GROSSET & DUNLAP, *Publishers*, NEW YORK

THE WESTY MARTIN BOOKS

By PERCY KEESE FITZHUGH

Author of the "Tom Slade" and "Roy Blakeley" Books, Etc.

Individual Colored Wrappers. Illustrated.
Every Volume Complete in Itself.

Westy Martin, known to every friend of Roy Blakeley, appears as the hero of adventures quite different from those in which we have seen him participate as a Scout of Bridgeboro and of Temple Camp. On his way to the Yellowstone the bigness of the vast West and the thoughts of the wild preserve that he is going to visit make him conscious of his own smallness and of the futility of "boy scouting" and woods lore in this great region. Yet he was to learn that if it had not been for his scout training he would never have been able to survive the experiences he had in these stories.

WESTY MARTIN

WESTY MARTIN IN THE YELLOWSTONE

WESTY MARTIN IN THE ROCKIES

WESTY MARTIN ON THE SANTA FE TRAIL

WESTY MARTIN ON THE OLD INDIAN TRAILS

GROSSET & DUNLAP, *Publishers*, NEW YORK

THE LITTLE WASHINGTONS SERIES

By LILLIAN ELIZABETH ROY

Handsomely Bound. Colored Wrappers. Illustrated.
For Children 6 to 12 Years

This series presents early American history in a manner that impresses the young readers. Because of George and Martha Washington Parke, two young descendants of the famous General Washington, these stories follow exactly the life of the great American, by means of playing they act the life of the Washingtons, both in battles and in society.

THE LITTLE WASHINGTONS

Their thrilling battles and expeditions generally end in "punishment" lessons read by Mrs. Parke from the "Life of Washington." The culprits listen intently, for this reading generally gives them new ideas for further games of Indian warfare and Colonists' battles.

THE LITTLE WASHINGTONS' RELATIVES

The Davis children visit the Parke home and join zealously in the games of playing General Washington. So zealously, in fact, that little Jim almost loses his scalp.

THE LITTLE WASHINGTONS' TRAVELS

The children wage a fierce battle upon the roof of a hotel in New York City. Then, visiting the Davis home in Philadelphia, the patriotic Washingtons vanquish the Hessians on a battle-field in the empty lot back of the Davis property.

THE LITTLE WASHINGTONS AT SCHOOL

After the school-house battle the Washingtons discover a band of gypsies camping near the back road to their homes and incidentally they secure the stolen horse which the gypsies had taken from the "butter and egg farmer" of the Parkes.

THE LITTLE WASHINGTONS' HOLIDAYS

They spend a pleasant summer on two adjoining farms in Vermont. During the voyage they try to capture a "frigate" but little Jim is caught and about to be punished by the Captain when his confederates hasten in and save him.

GROSSET & DUNLAP, PUBLISHERS, NEW YORK

Jerry Todd and Poppy Ott Series

BY LEO EDWARDS

Durably Bound. Illustrated. Individual Colored Wrappers.
Every Volume Complete in Itself.

Hundreds of thousands of boys who laughed until their sides ached over the weird and wonderful adventures of Jerry Todd and his gang demanded that Leo Edwards, the author, give them more books like the Jerry Todd stories with their belt-bursting laughs and creepy shivers. So he took Poppy Ott, Jerry Todd's bosom chum and created the Poppy Ott Series, and if such a thing could be possible— they are even more full of fun and excitement than the Jerry Todds.

THE POPPY OTT SERIES

POPPY OTT AND THE STUTTERING PARROT

POPPY OTT AND THE SEVEN LEAGUE STILTS

POPPY OTT AND THE GALLOPING SNAIL

POPPY OTT'S PEDIGREED PICKLES

THE JERRY TODD BOOKS

JERRY TODD AND THE WHISPERING MUMMY

JERRY TODD AND THE ROSE-COLORED CAT

JERRY TODD AND THE OAK ISLAND TREASURE

JERRY TODD AND THE WALTZING HEN

JERRY TODD AND THE TALKING FROG

JERRY TODD AND THE PURRING EGG

JERRY TODD IN THE WHISPERING CAVE

GROSSET & DUNLAP, Publishers, NEW YORK

CPSIA information can be obtained
at www.ICGtesting.com
Printed in the USA
BVHW041329060623
665472BV00002B/234